BOON
ON THE
MOON

JOHN HUDDLES

Boon On The Moon
The Booniverse: Book One
©2020 John Huddles
Notable Kids Publishing, LLC

ISBN 9780997085181 (Hardcover)

Library of Congress Control Number:2019952149
Huddles, John

Summary: When ten-year-old Byron "Boon" Barnett boards a rocket-ship for a move to the Moon with his family (and his irritating robot, José Ignacio), he's expecting the time of his life in the lunar colony of Cosmopolis. What he's *not* expecting is a stellar disaster that'll demolish Cosmopolis before lunch.

Mid-grade Fiction / Science Fiction / Fantasy (ages 8 +)

Printed in the United States of America.
Notable Kids Publishing, 8101 East Belleview, D1, Denver, CO 80237
303.850.5787 www.notablekidspublishing.com

Boon On The Moon
ISBN 978-1-7333548-8-2 (E-Book)

To GH

CHAPTER: 1

NOW PICTURE THIS: in an outer stretch of outer space, in the "cosmic deep" as the space-poets call it, in a quiet nook of the universe, a star explodes. This is a supernova: an astral bang which in an instant is shining a billion times brighter than our own sun.

The blast wave that follows slams hard into the first planet in this unlucky solar system. The planet slams into its moon, its moon slams into the next planet over, and so on and so forth until the wreckage from this celestial smash-up goes shooting every which way in a storm of newborn meteoroids.

But suddenly the supernova implodes, "imploding" being the opposite of "*exploding*," so instead of bursting further out, the supernova caves completely *in*. The star that used to be there is gone for good now, leaving in its place one of the strangest—and most dangerous—of all cosmic phenomena: a white worm.

Of course, the appearance of a white worm in an outer stretch of outer space would hardly matter to human beings such as us on any ordinary night, safe and snug in our beds a thousand galaxies away (though the ordinary is often an illusion while the hard-to-believe can be absolute fact). This story then begins properly in the bedroom of one Byron Barnett, nine years and eleven months old, an Arizonan born and bred, on a Thursday night at 7:35 p.m., or five minutes past Byron's school-night bedtime—though Byron was not in bed in the slightest.

The other members of the Barnett household were otherwise occupied at the moment and more or less unaware of

Byron's in-bed versus out-of-bed status. For instance: Byron's older brother, Taji, was downstairs in the den watching *Fear Sphere* on the telescreen, a show about people with unusual phobias. Tonight's episode: fear of smells and fear of being licked. Originally Taji's plan was to be out on a date, but his young lady had twisted her ankle playing laser-lacrosse earlier in the day and wasn't in the mood for any more excitement. So Taji had offered to stay in and babysit Byron—a term that Byron found highly offensive and visibly incorrect, since he hadn't been a baby for years.

By 7:36 p.m., Byron's father was standing in the foyer, looking in the wall mirror while folding a white handkerchief into the breast pocket of his tuxedo, after which he combed his hair, popped a mint in his mouth, and cleaned his glasses using a tissue from the fancy glass tissue box on the foyer table.

This takes us to 7:37 p.m., where two floors up, in Byron's bedroom, Byron was still not in bed. He had, at least, already pajamafied himself in his white flannels with the gold-colored stripes down the legs and golden shoulder patches, like the uniform for a soldier of sleep.

He also had on his Hat Of Many Dinosaurs, a feather-based creation that he'd made himself using imitation plumage and whatnot from the crafts and hobbies shop. It was an artist's impression in headwear of the kinds of feathers you would've seen on an assortment of dinosaurs if you'd been out for a stroll about a hundred million years before tonight. Byron found that most people didn't even know dinosaurs *had* feathers, which made the hat a real conversation-starter. On the downside, it had turned out to be more of a pre-sleep garment than an item you could wear to bed, since it was hard to lay your head on the pillow with so many feathers in the way. Byron had tried it more than once.

He was seated now at his card table next to the picture window, the window that he kept his telescope aimed through, the window with the best view of the Moon between the hours of dinner and slumber. In fact, earlier in the evening, Byron had devoted a good quarter hour to telescopically studying Crater Copernicus, one of the Moon's better indentations; but at the moment his eyes were fixed on the hand of cards he was holding in tonight's game of Flapjack.

Opposite him at the card table stood a robot of seven feet and several centimeters, its innards whirring faintly. Coincidentally, this mechanical individual, "José Ignacio" by name, had been constructed in the same color scheme as Byron's pajamas: metal casing the color of white flannel, with golden switches here and there for this and that. José Ignacio was the picture of card-playing competition, holding his own claw of cards close to his titanium torso.

Byron looked up at the robot's glass cranium and said: "Showdown."

Rotating his claw to reveal his cards, José Ignacio informed Byron dryly:

"Blueberry flush."

Byron grunted his irritation. "Pair of walnuts," he said, spreading his losing cards on the table.

From the staircase in the hallway came the voice of Mrs. Barnett:

"Byron? Are you in bed?"

"Very nearly!"

"Teeth brushed?"

"Yes, and I can prove it!"

"Toys, devices, and cards put away?"

"Not at the present nanosecond!"

Mrs. Barnett appeared in the doorway. She was dressed up for a night out, wearing a glittering red gown and fastening an earring in her ear. She eyed Byron at his card table—where he gave her an outstanding grin, if possibly one too wide for the size of his face.

"You haven't seen my red cape by any chance," she said.

"Ummmmmmmmmmm—I don't believe so. Not today."

Mrs. Barnett considered her son's odd answer for a moment. But since most of Byron's answers were, frankly, odder than this one, she decided not to pursue the question.

"I'm coming back in five minutes. Be in bed." She stepped out of the room, closing the door behind her.

Byron turned to José Ignacio across the card table and made a face like a person getting a flu shot.

"What's wrong?" José Ignacio said.

Byron loudly sucked in all the saliva in his mouth.

"What *is* it?" José Ignacio said.

"The cape."

"No! Do not even *tell* me you left it where I think you left it."

"I left it where you think."

"Impressive," José Ignacio said—though he almost certainly meant exactly the opposite.

"I'll just go *get* it."

"You don't have enough time."

"Of *course* I do, you outrageous apparatus!"

Byron leapt up from the card table and dashed into his walk-in closet. A moment later he came out jumping a leg into a sleek, silver spacesuit, complete with slim oxygen tank on the back.

"Your parents are about to leave!" José Ignacio said.

"You're not a problem-solver, José Ignacio! It's among your very greatest flaws!"

Byron put both hands on his tightly fitting hat and pushed it up and off, revealing a cobalt-blue head of hair underneath. Actually it was only about fifty-two percent cobalt-blue, since the pigment pills that Byron took once a week didn't change the natural black of every single one of his hairs. More like every other hair. But the two hues blended together nicely, akin to the sheen of a cobalt-blue tarantula—widely considered the one really gorgeous member of the spider family.

After giving his scalp a vigorous rub (because the feathers on the Hat of Many Dinosaurs tended to leave one's scalp quite itchy), Byron dropped to his knees and pulled out from under his bed a device on wheels. It was nearly as tall as Byron himself, cylindrical, about a foot in diameter, with spinning mechanical innards visible through its glass casing. Byron unspooled its electrical cord and plugged it into a wall socket.

José Ignacio grumbled: "I don't know how reliable a biomass transducer is from a mail-order company."

"Lunar Shipping Systems is a perfectly respectable outfit!"

"Says who?"

"Says their ad in *Lunar Life Quarterly*. Anyway, I've already used the thing a dozen times."

"And you still can't aim it. You could be off by half a mile."

"Then I'll run the rest of the way!"

"But there's a meteoroid storm in the forecast! It's too risky!"

"I giggle at risk! I give risk a kick in the shins!"

"You're saying two things at once. Which is it, you giggle or you kick?"

Putting on his spacesuit's clear bubble helmet, Byron's voice went muffled in answering:

"I giggle *then* I kick! Then I make risk do the dishes!"

As Byron latched down his helmet on both sides, José Ignacio extracted a stopwatch from a hidden compartment on his metallic elbow and started a countdown. "You have four minutes," he said. "I'm betting against you."

Byron switched on the biomass transducer: the device revved up fast with a sound like the drill at the dentist's. Next he opened one of the bedroom's tall windows. He peered through the transducer's built-in telescope and zeroed in first on the Moon itself, then more specifically on Crater Copernicus. He angled the transducer, getting the position as tight as he could for maximum trajectory. He detached from the transducer a remote control featuring a small joystick and a switch labeled for two settings: "Propulsion" and "Suction." He set the switch to "Propulsion." Positioning himself between the transducer and the open window (with the Moon perfectly framing his bubble-helmeted head), he sneered at José Ignacio and thumbed a button on the remote.

The transducer fired its propulsion beam straight into him, shooting him out the window and up into the night sky. It felt something like being kicked in the chest by a horse while an octopus tickled you under your arms and lathered your hair with carbonated shampoo all at the same time. Byron was half laughing, half shrieking as the transducer's beam pushed him two hundred and thirty-eight thousand, eight hundred and fifty-five miles between the Earth and Moon in just under ten seconds ...

He slammed into the lunar surface, sending up a cloud of moondust not unlike the talcum powder he enjoyed sprinkling over his feet after a bath. He lay still for a few seconds, recovering from the impact. The biomass transducer had its drawbacks. Byron wouldn't have admitted it to José Ignacio, but this was *not* the most reliable way to get to the Moon. Unfortunately the price of a ticket on a rocket-ship was several hundred times Byron's weekly allowance, possibly several thousand.

Anyway, rocket-ships only left from spaceports, and the biomass transducer had made off-Earth travel possible from the comfort of Byron's own bedroom—without anyone else having to know about it. How safe was the device really? Who knew? But Byron was no worrywart. Even the pain of a harsh lunar landing was not enough to put him off, since a little pain never hurt anybody in the pursuit of big things. Especially *this* big thing, the thing of being on the Moon, which was, to put it simply, Byron's great obsession, his ruling passion, his constant desire and self-assigned mission in life.

Jumping to his feet, he brushed the moondust off his spacesuit and scanned his surroundings. With the clock ticking, he figured he had approximately three minutes and forty-two seconds left to get the job done and get back to Earth. José Ignacio had been right about at least one thing: Byron still couldn't aim the transducer very well, so he was not now at his actual destination.

To get his bearings he tried orienting himself against the mile-high mountain range in the distance, its peaks all bright with starlight—but truth be told, this left him still slightly fuzzy on where he was. Fortunately the built-in compass on his spacesuit was in good working order. After checking it, he pivoted south and bounded off. In the low gravity it didn't take long to get to the rim of Crater Copernicus, that monumental indentation on the lunar surface that was some fifty-eight miles across and more than two miles deep.

Standing right on the edge, Byron leaned over and looked down. He contemplated, cogitated, and knew what

he had to do next. He switched on the miniature reel-to-reel
tape player built into his spacesuit, filling his helmet with his
favorite song of the moment, "Mucus," by his favorite band
of the year, Phlegm. He backed up several steps, ran straight
at the crater's edge, and jumped …

                                        …

                                   …

                              …

As he fell in low-gravity slo-mo down the double-mile drop,
he twisted onto his back so he could watch the stars swirling
above him …

               …

          …

… then flipped onto his stomach to see the crater floor rushing up below …

               ……

               …………

… until, right before impact, he jabbed the release-button
on his wrist—and an airbag like a cluster of fifty beach balls
burst from his spacesuit's chest compartment to cushion his
fall. The impact knocked the wind out of him anyway, but
he was alive, he was on the floor of the crater, and he was in
one piece.

    The airbag deflated automatically, after which he detached
and discarded it. Next he swiveled toward the middle of the
crater and started running. He was making good time, charging
toward his target (it helped that Phlegm was thumping out a
beat for him with the drum solo in "Mucus"). But then, in his
peripheral vision he noticed objects streaking overhead, which
wasn't only inconvenient, it was especially irksome, because it
meant there was another thing that José Ignacio had been right
about: the meteoroid storm.

Suddenly space-rocks were coming down in every direction. One landed directly ahead of Byron and blasted a mini-crater-within-a-crater out of the lunar surface. Another landed to his left and blew a boulder to bits. A third hit the powdery surface and rolled like a gigantic bowling ball right past him. Zigzagging to avoid being hit himself, Byron started laughing in a kind of crazy glee, enjoying the bombardment more than made sense …

… until he tripped and conked his head inside his helmet, which sucked the fun out of the whole thing. He jumped up, shook it off, and dashed toward the goal of this entire operation: his lunar fort, at the crater's dead center. The size and shape of a largish igloo, the fort was made of foot-thick super-glass and featured a flagpole rising over it, flying a red flag with a skull and crossbones in masking tape.

This is why Byron was here, because the red flag, in actual fact, was a red cape, his mother's red cape, which he'd borrowed from her closet and brought up to the Moon the week before. He'd wanted to see if he would like the look of a red flag over his fort before saving up several weeks' allowance to buy a *real* one. As it turned out, he'd liked the look of it very much; but then, regrettably, he'd forgotten to bring it home with him.

Still darting sideways and once or twice backwards to dodge incoming meteoroids, Byron moved toward his destination as best he could. It was more a dance than a dash at this point, but such is life. When the meteoroid storm let up a little, he capitalized on the opening to lunge for the fort, where he jumped onto an adjacent boulder, sprang off it in a low-gravity leap, flew right up to the very top of the flagpole, and grabbed hold.

He curled his spacesuited legs around the pole and stationed himself there. With his hands freed up, he began untying the cape from the crosspiece that stretched it out and held it in place. Once the crucial garment was in his possession, he dropped down to the curved roof of the fort, hopped off to the lunar surface, and dashed *into* the fort, closing the little airlock tightly behind him. Here he unzipped the front of his spacesuit and started stuffing in the cape, in preparation for the trip home. The suit's fabric was just stretchy enough to fit the whole cape in, though getting the zipper closed was a challenge.

After this was done, he scanned the fort for signs of intruders. Fortunately everything looked the way he'd left it last time: orange leather recliner ready to be reclined in (just not today) ... telescope aimed at the rings of Saturn ... recent editions of *Lunar Life Quarterly* in a stack on the side table ... half-full box of Space Gazelle Space Cakes on the shelf. It was a variety pack, so Byron reached in with eyes closed and by pure luck picked his favorite flavor: Chocolate Comet.

As a wholly owned subsidiary of Galactic Snacking Solutions Incorporated, Space Gazelle truly was one of today's great food-and-beverage brands, in Byron's opinion. Also he enjoyed their mascot, the Gazelle, pictured on all the packaging—a gazelle being a kind of slender antelope. *This* gazelle, the Space Gazelle, wore a spacesuit that even covered his upward-curving horns—so presumably he was having miscellaneous adventures out in the cosmic deep. Byron hadn't been able to track down any of the details on that, though he'd written to Galactic Snacking Solutions asking for information.

Anyway: the Space Cakes. Byron could live on them if he had to. They were actually *too* tasty, which is why he'd decided to only keep them here in his fort instead of at home in the kitchen pantry along with the rest of his provisions. If the Cakes were as easy to get to as a quick trip downstairs, he'd polish off a box every couple of days. Better to leave them way up here on the Moon, where he could only eat them on intermittent lunar occasions.

Not to imply that they were bad for you. Space Gazelle snacks were extremely wholesome across their entire product line, as Byron had to keep explaining to his mother every time they went to the grocery store together. Not only were the Space Cakes packed with protein from almonds and other delicious nuts, but right on the wrapper it stated:

"For Astronomical Energy!"

What more could you ask from a foodstuff? Yet Space Gazelle *gave* you more: they put extra calcium and Vitamin D in everything they made, nutrients your body needs when you're living extraterrestrially: on the Moon or in a space station or aboard a rocket-ship intercepting an asteroid.

Sadly, in Byron's experience adults failed to appreciate the role that snacks played in getting you through the day, whether on Earth or elsewhere. Life was hard; refreshments helped— *especially* in space. And if appetites were sometimes spoiled between meals, such was the price one paid for being human.

In fact, Byron's backup plan to becoming an officer in the Astral Corps and piloting rocket-ships across the cosmos was being President and CEO of Space Gazelle Brands— because surely whoever was head of the company right now would be ready to retire by the time Byron was old enough for the job. Or if not Space Gazelle, then he might even start a competing operation of his own. He was confident that he could add value to the future of snacking.

Just thinking about it made him feel like he needed a nibble, even though his teeth were brushed and apart from the fact that he was on the Moon, he was supposed to be in bed. Unlatching and taking off his helmet, he ripped open the Cake's foil wrapper, crammed the whole thing in his mouth, and chewed fast. His mother often told him to slow down with his food, but looking up through the fort's glass roof he could see that the meteoroid storm was still going strong—and one rather jumbo-sized rock was heading his way.

Gulping his Cake—not so easy without a glass of chilled hazelnut milk to wash it down—he re-helmeted and scrambled out the door mere seconds before the fort was hit by the incoming meteoroid—and demolished. Only when he was a good twenty yards away and out of range of flying chunks of smashed super-glass did he stop running.

Here he unclipped the biomass transducer's remote control from his spacesuit belt, switched its setting from "Propulsion" to "Suction," pushed a button, and watched a suction beam shoot from the Earth up to his vicinity here on the Moon. But it was still aimed at the spot *above* Crater Copernicus where he'd landed—two miles straight up the crater.

With more meteoroids bombing the moonscape all around him, Byron worked his remote's little joystick, causing the suction beam in the distance to swivel in his direction. He only had a few seconds of leeway, however, because a space-rock with his name on it was screeching down from the storm and would surely crack him open like a piñata, sending his blood, guts, and gore spilling over the lunar surface if he didn't—

CONTACT! The suction beam snatched Byron up and off the Moon half a heartbeat before the incoming meteoroid smacked him dead, yanking him home at just under 27,000 miles per second. He shot through the open window of his bedroom, hit the floor, and rolled uncontrollably until he slammed into the far wall—which brought him to a stop.

José Ignacio, still seated at the card table, looked up from his magazine, *Good Semiconducting,* eyed Byron, and clicked his stopwatch. Six seconds remained on the clock: Byron had transduced to the Moon and back in under four minutes. It was a solid victory, but before the robot could comment one way or the other, Byron unzipped his spacesuit, pulled out the red cape, and waved it in triumph.

Not thirty seconds later Mrs. Barnett opened the door from the hallway, holding her red cape. She glared at Byron in bed.

"Byron Barnett: why was my cape hanging on your doorknob?"

"I found it for you!"

His mother gave him a cold stare, so Byron added:

"You're welcome!"

For a moment Mrs. Barnett was distracted by Byron's blue hair, which looked even bluer than usual against the bright white of a freshly laundered pillow case. She still didn't understand why a soon-to-be ten-year-old would spend half his weekly allowance on pigment pills that changed his hair from its normal human black to the color of a peacock's neck—or as Byron liked to remind her, the sheen of a cobalt-blue tarantula. But their pediatrician had assured them the pills were perfectly safe, so there wasn't anything to object to on medical grounds. And at least Byron was keeping his hair combed for a change, so that was a plus.

Mrs. Barnett looked around Byron's room now with an exploratory eye, as moms are wont to do, until something by the card table caught her attention. "And what is *that* doing up here?" she said.

"My biomass transducer?"

"Yes, Byron, your 'biomass transducer.' Or as I like to call it: my vacuum cleaner."

Now Mrs. Barnett saw something *else* she didn't like and crossed the room to pick it up off the floor. It was Byron's Halloween costume from last year, a silver spacesuit, complete with plastic bubble helmet and pretend oxygen tank. She draped it over the clothes valet in the corner and informed Byron that throwing one's things on the floor was a sign of general disrespect about the things one was lucky enough to have. And to *have* things at the age of nine and eleven months, one had to be *given* things—by one's parents. One could always be given—did it really need to be said out loud?—less.

But if his spacesuit was a Halloween costume and his bio-mass transducer a vacuum cleaner, what did that mean about Byron's quick trip to the Moon of a moment ago? It meant that Byron had only been to the Moon in his mind, a sad fact he would have done anything in his power to change.

What had happened in reality was this: wearing his Halloween costume and with his mother's vacuum cleaner whirling its mood-setting sound, Byron had climbed out his window, down the emergency ladder drilled into the glass polygons of the house, and into the garden. From there he'd dashed into the desert just *behind* the house, zigzagging around cactuses whose spines and spikes could've pierced his pajamas and slashed his skin if he'd accidentally made contact at the speed he was going, since even the light from the Moon wasn't always enough to see by in the desert after dark.

About fifty yards from the house he'd reached his fort, a structure the size of a large shed, made of junked materials that Byron's brother had been good enough to acquire for him from a hovercraft body shop in town. *Above* the fort, Mrs. Barnett's red cape was hooked atop an old telescreen antenna that looked like a metal fern, the cape not flying there magnificently flag-like, but drooped like a dead flower in the windless night. Byron had yanked it down, dashed with it back to the house, climbed the ladder up to and then through his bedroom window, hung the cape on the door-knob in the hallway, pulled off his Halloween costume (he was still wearing his pajamas underneath), and jumped into bed. Which is where he now lay, watching his mother roll her vacuum cleaner toward him from the other side of the room. She stopped beside him and stared down.

"What is it doing up here?" she asked again.

"I was cleaning!" Byron said.

Mrs. Barnett looked around. "I see no proof of that."

Byron tried to make his eyes sparkle by angling his face under the bedside lamp, but his mother seemed immune to his every charm tonight.

"And where specifically did you 'find' my cape?" she wanted to know.

"You look pretty! Red is your color!"

"You're too kind," Mrs. Barnett said suspiciously. She bent down, tucked Byron's blanket tightly around his sides, mummifying him the way he liked. Then she kissed his forehead and turned toward the door. Which is when Byron saw something frightening.

"Wait!"

His mother stopped. "Yes?"

"One more kiss!"

Mrs. Barnett stepped back in, bent down again, and gave Byron another kiss, during which Byron used the end of his blanket to pluck a tiny cactus ball off the red cape in his mother's hand. It would've been a nasty turn of events for all concerned if, wearing her cape out on the town tonight, she'd sat down on a cactus-balled bit of it.

At the door again Mrs. Barnett stopped one last time, glanced back at Byron, then over at Byron's twelve-inch toy robot on its stool at the card table—gripping five full-sized playing cards in its tiny claw—then back at Byron.

"Go to sleep," she said firmly—and closed the door behind her.

So we come, at last, to a crucial clarification: the robot José Ignacio was not, strictly speaking, real. At least not the seven-foot-and-several-centimeters José Ignacio that weighed three hundred and thirty-three pounds and forty-four grams. The life-sized José Ignacio, to say it another way, was a figment of Byron's brain.

As soon as his mother was gone, Byron turned to the seven-foot José Ignacio at the card table and said:

"What's the moral of this story?"

"Never share a bedroom with a demented person?"

"Wrong! Never bet against a person who thinks being demented is a *good* thing, you bulbous widget!"

"Why don't I feel this is the end of The Incident of The Missing Red Cape?"

"Because you're a catastrophizer! And I'm an optimist! That's the difference between us!"

"I'm too tired to fight about it," José Ignacio grumbled, crossing the room from the card table to the second twin bed. "I'm powering down now for a circuit purge."

"Congratulations."

Byron turned away from the robot and stared out the window at the Moon. What a killjoy José Ignacio was. Still, the robot's track record for being right about things was annoyingly good.

Thinking about it, Byron's natural optimism decayed by several iotas as he drifted into sleep ...

Meanwhile, a thousand galaxies from Byron's bedroom, way out in what used to be that quiet nook of the universe but was now the cosmic zip code of a certain monstrous white worm, extreme things were happening.

First a quick description of the worm itself: five thousand miles long, its front end was a dark, round, swirling mouth ... its middle section was bright white like a fluorescent light bulb, but stretchable like the hose on a vacuum cleaner ... and its back end ended in an electrified coil that was already starting to zap its way through the very fabric of space.

From every direction *around* the worm space-rubble was at this moment hurtling toward it. No surprise really, since the gravitational field of a white worm is one of the strongest forces in nature, so strong that nothing it swallows can ever escape again: not a comet, not a spaceship, not even a beam of light. (These items might eventually be pooped out the worm's *other* end, but that's a whole different discussion.)

Also: random rays of gravitation were firing out from this particular white worm, sticking onto more distant objects and yanking them in the way a frog's long tongue catches flies. For instance, the trillion-ton chunk of a smashed-up moon had just been yanked at six hundred miles a second toward the worm's swirling mouth. On contact it had simply vanished, like some astral magic trick—exactly the kind of trick that Byron himself would have loved to see, if he'd had a telescope with intergalactic magnification and known where to point it.

Actually he'd never even heard of a white worm: this was a gap in his space-education that would be fixed sooner rather than later. For the moment though, in a deep sleep with nothing wormy whatsoever on his mind, he was dreaming about having just won a quiz show by correctly answering the question:

Dinosaur feathers: true or false?

… his prize being a lifetime supply of Space Gazelle Space Cakes—all of which made for some very pleasant slumber and was sure to leave him hungry by the time he woke up.

The next morning at the breakfast table, Mr. Barnett was finishing off his egg-white omelette with Spanish seasonings, Mrs. Barnett was spooning elegantly at her grapefruit and yoghurt, Taji was enjoying his bowl of buttery oatmeal, and Byron was deeply engaged in a plate of chocolate-chip waffles. So engaged that he was taken completely by surprise when his mother turned to him and said:

"I had an interesting experience with my cape last night."

Byron's heart jumped in his chest. Had he missed another cactus ball? Had his mother sat down wearing the cape in a restaurant and jumped up howling from a barb in the buttock? Had an ambulance been called and the emergency room visited? Were stitches involved? Was his mother wearing a bandage under her skirt at this very moment?

"Your father and I were walking out of the theatre," Mrs. Barnett continued.

"What did you see?" Taji asked.

"*The Importance of Being Earnest,*" Mr. Barnett said. "A fine production."

"And just at the bottom of the staircase," Mrs. Barnett said, "there was a commotion in the crowd behind us. Sort of a surge of whispering and snickering."

Mr. Barnett focused an intense eyeball on Byron—and Byron, though he had no idea what was coming next, knew it wasn't going to be anything good.

"So we turned around," Mrs. Barnett said, "and saw that the commotion was all about *me*. People were chattering and laughing, and some were even pointing. At my back. To be precise about it: at the back of my cape. During the show I'd used my purse pen to write down an idea that popped into my head for a pumpkin soufflé, and I thought maybe I'd held the pen against the folded cape in my lap and it had leaked. But it wasn't ink on my cape."

"It wasn't?" Byron said.

"No, it wasn't. It was masking tape."

"*Mask*ing tape?" echoed Taji.

"Masking tape," confirmed Mrs. Barnett. "In the shape of a skull and crossbones. I looked like a big red flag on a pirate ship."

"Not a *pirate* ship!" Byron blurted, "a lunar *fort*! To warn space-vermin to steer clear!"

Mr. Barnett put down his fork. "Byron, please explain what you were doing with your mother's cape without permission in the first place."

Answering a somewhat different question, Byron insisted:

"I didn't *mean* to leave it on the Moon! I just forgot to bring it *back* with me last time I was there! Then when I transduced up last night to get it, I forgot to peel off the skull and crossbones before I hung it on the doorknob. I'm sorry!"

Calmly Mrs. Barnett told him:

"I don't mind being laughed at by people I don't know, Byron. No one should worry *too* much about what other people think of them. But *if* I'm going to be laughed at, I'd prefer it to be for something *I've* decided to do: like taking a fashion risk that hasn't paid off or standing up for something I believe in that other people find ridiculous or even because I've slipped on a banana peel and fallen on my fundament. What I *don't* especially care for is being laughed at because of a risk *you've* decided to take that affects me without my knowledge. And above all, I don't appreciate being embroiled in an unpleasant situation as the result of a half-truth, falsehood, or fantasy of any sort."

"If it makes you feel better," Byron said, "your cape *did* look really good as a moon-flag. Now I know that an actual red flag is what I want to fly there."

Mrs. Barnett shook her head and turned to her husband. Mr. Barnett was equally displeased. "Where, Byron," he asked, "is the dividing line?"

"Between what and what?"

"Between using your imagination for fun and using it as an excuse for bad behavior."

"Um … is that a real question?"

"It's a question I want you to spend some time thinking about. You're going to be ten years old next month. Telling the truth should not be optional by age ten. Remember: veracity, or the quality of being honest—with yourself *and* with other people—is the hallmark of a first-rate person. On the other hand, being 'mendacious,' which is the quality of being *un*truthful as a general rule, is something that one way or another will ruin your life in the end."

Byron scrunched up his face and nodded slowly to convey his understanding of this vital point that his father was making—though a fair bit of scrunch was really about the breakfast-related tragedy that his chocolate-chip waffles were going cold.

CHAPTER: 2

TWENTY-FOUR AND A HALF HOURS LATER, or Saturday morning at 8:10 a.m., Byron lay awake in bed, his gaze fixed upward on a particularly impressive pinwheel galaxy in a corner of a map of the universe laminated across his ceiling. His mind was therefore light-years away from the here and now when the intercom on his night table chimed, and his mother's voice sang through it pleasantly:

"*Break*fast!"

Byron sprang out of bed like a boy on a coil and began pulling off his pajamas (this time he was wearing the electric purple ones with the silver comets).

"Get up!" he barked at José Ignacio, who was lying inert in the second twin bed. "We're on a tight schedule!"

"I'm resting my diodes," José Ignacio said. "Check back with me around eleven."

Byron charged over and tried yanking his robotic associate into an upright position, but with José Ignacio weighing three hundred and thirty-three pounds and forty-four grams, the yanking had little physical effect. It was, on the other hand, seriously annoying.

"Get *up*!" Byron said.

"Get *off* me, you driveling idiot!" José Ignacio snapped back.

Byron persisted. Finally José Ignacio raised a claw and zapped his tormentor with a low-dose voltage-ray. Byron yelped, backed off, and warned in a menacing voice:

"That was unwise."

He reached for the plastic sword that hung over his desk and darted across the room swinging. A duel ensued, Byron smacking José Ignacio with his plastic blade, José Ignacio retaliating for every sword strike with a voltage-ray that felt like bee stings on Byron's arms and knuckles and one well-aimed zap on the tip of his nose.

In the clash of four-foot boy versus seven-foot robot, Byron's most notable quality, apart from his daring, was his cunning. When tossed by José Ignacio back onto his own bed, Byron swiped a handful of magnets off the magnetic bulletin board over the night table and flung them at the robot's sensitive underarm area. A few bounced right off, but a bunch stuck onto José Ignacio as planned, sending him into mechanical spasms, the robotic version of hiccups.

Now Byron had his opening. He rushed José Ignacio—and tackled him to the floor. If the house hadn't been so well-built, the force of three hundred and thirty-three pounds and forty-four grams of industrial-grade titanium slamming onto the carpet might've done real damage to the floorboards underneath. But the Barnett house was of sturdy construction. This was the reason the brawling twosome didn't go crashing through wood and wiring and plaster, or at least this was the reason for it in Byron's mind.

Byron was now straddling José Ignacio, working him into a chokehold.

"Get *up*, you oversized utensil!"

José Ignacio did not comply.

"You're gonna get up and get going this second or I'm turning you off!"

With his pinkie Byron reached for the power switch on José Ignacio's neck; but José Ignacio got a claw around Byron's wrist and held him at bay. They were locked in stalemate—struggling, grunting, and Byron's nose starting to drip—when from the intercom on the night table came the voice of Mrs. Barnett:

"Byron? What are you doing up there?"

The combatants eyed each other as Mrs. Barnett added: *"I have French toast with your name written all over it!"*

Byron leapt downstairs dressed in his Saturday khakis, though carrying rather than wearing his silver sneakers. He often preferred leaping to walking, especially through the long, bamboo-floored hallways of his house, which made for extremely good sliding between leaps so long as the leaper wore socks but no shoes. Also it was quite agreeable to whiz in this way past the rocky red terrain outside, since the house, built of stacked glass polygons, offered vistas galore.

But the best thing to look at through the glass was the garden. Byron's mother's garden: a triumph of xeriscaping, which means landscaping without using water. (Or using very little of it.) *This* xeriscape was a fantasyland of succulent plants, meaning your aloes, your agaves, and your cactuses (though some people like to say "cacti"—nobody really knows which word is right)—all framed by a "backyard" of desert that ran to the canyons on the horizon.

Mrs. Barnett was, let's just be clear about it, a genius of the gardening arts, the same way she was a genius of the arts domestic. Basically everything in and around the house got better whenever she got involved. Even something as routine as breakfast, where she could've relied on her gadgetry to do the job in the usual way—using her laser-toaster, her sonic eggbeater, her auto-griddle and her scanning electron oven— even here, she always added her own, extra-specially artistic touch.

For example: the plate of French toast that she set down now for Byron, who'd just slid into his seat and slapped a napkin over his lap. Not only was this sure to be a master-piece in the mouth of bread, butter, honey, egg, and spice—but Mrs. Barnett had written the letters "B-Y-R-O-N" over the top slice using a stencil and powdered sugar.

"Thanks, mom!"

"You're most welcome."

Byron pronged a whole slice with his fork. Lifting utensil to lips, he realized he should've cut the slice in half first, but decided to stuff it all in anyway.

With bulging cheeks, he watched his mother begin filling the dishwasher, hoping she wouldn't turn around and see him chomping his food. But even trying his best, he still couldn't swallow the whole lump in his throat and had to swig his entire glass of pineapple juice as a liquid plunger.

Byron's brother suddenly sprinted into the kitchen, calling ahead:

"Sorry, mom, gotta eat quick! I'm late for a date!"

Mrs. Barnett whirled from the dishwasher. "Who has a date at eight in the morning?"

"Whoever can get one!"

Taji offered his mother a wicked grin. Mrs. Barnett shook her head at him, but you could tell she wasn't really bothered.

Sometimes Byron failed to understand the things that his brother and parents found so amusing, usually when the subject under discussion was—Byron disliked the very word—"romance." Unfortunately the subject had been coming up quite a lot lately, because Taji Barnett, at the age of sixteen, was a young man concerned mostly with young ladies. The young ladies generally didn't mind the attention, because Taji was hunky, Taji was jolly, Taji was funny, and Taji had wit. He could make conversation as easily as popping open a bottle of strawberry soda and pouring everybody a glass. The very words he used bubbled and frothed. By comparison, witty words and how to use them to amuse female individuals held specifically zero interest for Byron. Just one of the ways in which he and his brother had nothing in common.

Not only in personality but even in appearance the Brothers Barnett were as different as chocolate and broccoli, though looks-wise the difference was almost certainly because Taji was adopted. Byron had been born ten minutes away at the Arizona Memorial Medical Center. Taji had been born in a hospital halfway around the planet, in the city of Nairobi, in the African country of Kenya—where Mr. and Mrs. Barnett had gone to pick him up when he was only two months old.

Taji's biological parents had slipped up to heaven quite early, but they'd written in their will that Mr. and Mrs. Barnett, who'd been their best friends in engineering school and best man and matron of honor at their wedding, should come collect their kid if ever he needed a new mom and dad. So that's just what the Barnetts did.

Taji's full name, by the way, was Taji Lindmark Mwangi Barnett, the Mwangis being his father's family back in Africa and the Lindmarks his mother's Swedish clan from the Scandinavian Confederation. Byron himself had more of a Spanish-y set of middle names, on account of his mother being born and raised in South America, in the country of Colombia. He was officially Byron Benedicto Timoteo Valiente Barnett. "Benedicto" after his mom's dad. "Timoteo" after his mom's favorite cousin. And "Valiente" for no reason in particular.

Unlike many people, Byron didn't mind his middle names, though he felt that his brother's original last name from the Swahili language, "Mwangi," had the most gracious

ring to it out of all the names in the family, which is why
he'd recently asked his parents if they'd consider letting him
legally change his *own* name to Byron Benedicto Timoteo
Valiente Mwangi Barnett.

They'd said probably not. A missed opportunity, Byron
thought. Especially since it would've let him get an I.D. card
to prove to people he really *was* Taji's brother. Because whenever Byron and Taji went out anywhere together, no one ever
guessed, and only occasionally believed it when told, that
they were related. Byron was a touch on the short side even
for age nine and eleven months, while Taji was on the tall
end of the teenage spectrum.

Also: Taji was so handsome that every time he walked
through the mall at City Center, one of the lady department-
store managers always ran up to ask if he'd be a male model
at their next fashion show. And of course Taji's girlfriends
were always talking about his "delicious curls of dark blond
hair," a bonus effect of his Swedish-Kenyan genetic blend
(though Byron *still* didn't get how hair could be delicious);
not to mention what the girls called Taji's "drop-dead com-
plexion" (whatever that meant); and his "muscly arms"
(okay, that one at least made sense); and his "coffee-colored
eyes" (which sounded to Byron like a stupid way to describe
a color—because what if you put *cream* in your coffee?).

When anyone commented on *Byron's* looks, it was usually
José Ignacio, and more often than not, not a compliment.
Nothing like what people or machines said about Taji. But
despite all these differences, and even with the large gap in
age and height, the Barnett boys genuinely enjoyed each
other's company and expected to be friends for life. And
really, what more can two brothers ask for than that?

"Boon, please pass the syrup."

"Boon" was the nickname for Byron that Taji himself had come up with when Byron was only one week old. Byron had always quite liked this moniker and often wondered how he could get other people to start using it when referring to him. He was about to bring up the subject again when his father came down the back stairwell connecting the kitchen to the master bedroom. Mr. Barnett was wearing his brown houndstooth suit and fumbling at his necktie, which he wasn't very good at tying even in front of the mirror, let alone while navigating the stairs. He looked to his wife and said:

"The office just called. They need me to come in right away."

"On a Saturday?"

"Maybe they're firing you!" guessed Byron, his mouth crammed with another slice of French toast.

"Byron!" said Mrs. Barnett. "Of *course* they're not firing your father. He's the best engineer in the history of the company!"

"Thank you, my love," said Mr. Barnett, "but let's not embellish." He turned to Byron and clarified: "*Second* best in the history of the company."

"Either way," said Mrs. Barnett, "I can't imagine what was so urgent that they had to interrupt your weekend."

"Mine is not to reason why, mine is but to do or die."

"Well, *I'll* die if you go in looking like you were dressed by an orangutang."

Reaching for her husband's tie, she undid its bungled knot and began it again. Mr. Barnett, meanwhile, took off his eyeglasses and rubbed them against his sleeve, losing focus on everything around him.

"How did I ever convince a goddess to marry me?" he said to the beautiful blur of his wife's face.

"By promising her a lifetime of diamonds and roses," Mrs. Barnett reminded him.

"Ah. Good thing she understood my devilish sense of humor."

Mr. Barnett put his glasses back on as Mrs. Barnett finished off his tie with a tug. Husband and wife eyed each other in the silent amusement that powered so much of their time together; then Mr. Barnett kissed his wife on the nose.

"Step back," Mrs. Barnett said. "Let me get a good look at you to be sure nothing else is off-kilter."

Mr. Barnett took a step back, but really only so he could get a good look at Mrs. Barnett. After nineteen years of marriage, Wallace Barnett still found the former Bianca Barcelona the most gorgeous girl he'd ever known. He adored her dark brown eyes, her wavy black hair, her bright white teeth. She was, as he often told her, his "Latina Suprema." (Mrs. Barnett had been kind enough never to mention that the rhyme only worked if you were pronouncing the words in English, but didn't sound especially rhymey when you said it the right way in Spanish.)

Also Mr. Barnett loved the way Mrs. Barnett dressed. Today was classic Bianca: she wore a pink cashmere sweater set, a bright cherry cashmere skirt, and rose-gold earrings in the shape of starbursts.

From the kitchen table, after gulping down the last of his eggs Florentine, Taji said:

"Pops, if you're going past City Center, I could use a ride. You'd be saving me monorail fare."

"Snap to it then. The second your mother gives me the go-ahead, I'm out the door. Byron Barnett, what are *your* plans for the day?"

"I'll be spelunking," Byron announced.

Byron's parents and brother went stiff, like a bag of flash-frozen mixed vegetables.

("Spelunking," meaning the exploration of caves, was a word that Byron had recently found in the dictionary. He was fairly sure that using it now would show his parents how serious and, more to the point, how scientific he was about his cave work, and that understanding as much they'd give him their blessing to keep at it. This is not what happened.)

"Does it truly need to be pointed out," Mrs. Barnett said, "that you're still too young to be 'spelunking' at all, much less 'spelunking' on your own?"

"I'm not on my own, I have José Ignacio."

Byron gestured toward José Ignacio standing beside the kitchen counter, tall as the refrigerator, his power source emitting its distinctive if faint buzz.

The Barnetts all turned in the direction of Byron's gesture, but saw, as usual, only a twelve-inch toy robot on the countertop.

Mr. Barnett crossed the kitchen and reached down to press a button on the toy robot's little head, causing a bulb the size of a thimble inside its clear plastic cranium to light up. Nevertheless, from where Byron sat, and seen through Byron's eyes, his father had just reached *up* to press a button on the seven-foot-plus José Ignacio, causing a bulb as large as an orange to light up inside the equally transparent cranium of safety glass on the full-sized automaton.

Mr. Barnett turned back toward Byron at the kitchen table and said:

"When a boy of nine has only his robot—

"I'll be ten in twenty-six days," Byron interrupted.

Mr. Barnett paused, regarded his son calmly for a moment—because by nature he was a calm and collected type of dad—and started again:

"When a boy of ten minus twenty-six days has only his robot for a companion in a hundred square miles of open desert, a certain unavoidable peril is the result."

"I ridicule peril!" claimed Byron. "Ha-*ha*!"

"The last time you ridiculed peril was not a good day for the Barnett family."

"Last time I was climbing up a *cliff*, this time I'll be very gently lowering myself down into a *cave*."

"Last time you broke three bones."

"I can't stop gravity!"

"You lay there for an hour before anyone knew you were hurt."

"But I have my transponder now!"

He flapped his arm to emphasize a device resembling a wristwatch that he wore; but this was no timepiece.

"Your father made you that transponder to call for rescue in case of another emergency," said Mrs. Barnett, "not to give you permission to go looking for another emergency to be rescued *from*."

"But it's Saturday! What else am I supposed to do?"

"I think it's a good day to practice the violin."

Byron gasped as if some species of vicious monkey had snuck up behind him and bit him on the neck, though his mother was only following through on an agreement they'd made.

"Didn't we decide when you skipped your lesson last week to go to the movies with your brother that you'd make up the time on your own?" she said.

"But it was *My Teacher Was A Creature*! Anybody who knows anything about the history of the cinema knows it's one of the most significant motion pictures ever made!"

In Byron's mind flashed an image of himself in the packed movie house several days earlier, seated between Taji and Taji's date. Just now on-screen a teacher in a chemistry lab was morphing into a many-tentacled monster as he (or should we say "it") crept up on an unsuspecting kid looking through a microscope for an extra-credit assignment. With the horror unfolding to excruciating perfection, Byron grabbed the hands on either side of him: Taji's and the young lady's who'd come with them—until Taji whispered:

"You're breaking my fingers!"

—Byron snapped out of his little reverie and insisted to his mother:

"We're talking about quite possibly the greatest spine-chiller of all time! It only comes to the big screen every couple of years! I *had* to go see it!"

"Which is why we let you skip your violin lesson. And in return you promised to fit in an extra several hours of practice at home. In this house we keep *all* our promises, not merely the convenient ones."

Byron turned to his father for relief.

"Don't look at *me*," Mr. Barnett said, "I answer to *her*. Anyway, after the incident with your mother's cape Thursday night, I'm not sure this is the weekend for you to be getting a free pass."

"But what's the point of living in Arizona if a person can't survey the canyons and spelunk the caves? I'm an explorer! I was born to roam free!"

"Not today you weren't," said Mrs. Barnett. And with that the discussion was done.

From the long glass wall facing west in his third-floor bedroom, Byron watched morosely as his father settled into the driver's seat of the family's bubble-topped sedan. Mr. Barnett then lowered his window and called over to Taji just as Taji was leaving the house:

"I'm low on chloro-fuel—could you juice up a pint!"

Taji swerved onto the front lawn, bent down and ripped up a handful of grass. Stepping into the garage, he placed the grass in the intake port of the Liquimatic—an appliance the size of a Space Gazelle vending machine—and waited as a beaker in the dispenser port began to fill with green fluid. When the fluid reached the pint point, Taji carried the beaker out to the car, poured its contents into the fuel tank, then opened the passenger door and hopped in. The chloro-phyll-powered sedan motored away, its tailpipe burping the occasional green bubble as it went, the sole by-product of this clean-burning driving machine.

Mrs. Barnett stood at the front door waving her husband and son off. No sooner had they disappeared around the corner boulder than the letter carrier appeared in the sky, traveling by flight-pack. He landed at the far end of the Barnetts' driveway: it was Postal Service policy to touch down at least ten yards away from any homeowner, to avoid accidents in case of bad aim. He proceeded on foot to Mrs. Barnett, handed over the Barnetts' mail out of his satchel, chatted momentarily, and lifted off again to carry on with his route.

Byron crossed to the glass wall on the other side of his room, facing east, towards open desert. Putting an eye to his telescope, he surveyed the terrain of canyons and chasms that he considered by rights his weekend domain.

"How revolting: a perfectly good Saturday going to waste. Today was ideal for spelunking Devil's Drop Cave. It could be the long-lost underground on-ramp to an interdimensional highway for all anybody knows. Or maybe it goes straight down to the Earth's liquid core. Obviously *somebody's* got to investigate it."

He turned around for a supporting opinion from José Ignacio, who was again reclining in bed. But instead of answering, the robot pulled a blanket up to his neck.

"Are you listening to me?" Byron said.

"Not really."

"Why *not*?"

"Because you're exhausting me! You should stop grumbling and start practicing! Try a lullaby. I'm in the mood for a nap."

Byron reached for his violin and launched into "Flight Of The Bumblebee," quite likely the most irritating piece of music ever composed. Aiming to stir up trouble with José Ignacio, he was disappointed when the audio slots on the sides of the robot's cranium slid shut. So he gave up and began practicing scales.

At the same time, twenty miles away, Mr. Barnett's sedan streaked off the freeway, zipped beneath a monorail that was curling overhead, and shot toward the skyscape of Arizona City. First stop: the pavilion at City Center, a cluster of bistros and boutiques where the town's teenagers liked to meet up.

Mr. Barnett let Taji out at the soda shop. Taji walked up to the window and peeked in to see if his date was here yet—when something hit him hard across the buttocks, like a whack from a giant spatula. He whirled around to find his date smiling at him, looking sharp in her laser-lacrosse uniform (she had a game later that morning) and twirling the lacrosse stick that she'd just whacked him with.

Mr. Barnett, meanwhile, was already on the road again, though it was only a short drive to his office, a two-hundred-floor skyscraper topped with the name of its anchor tenant in ten-foot-tall neon letters—the anchor tenant that also happened to be the company where Mr. Barnett worked: Amalgamated MegaPhysics.

He sped into the underground parking structure, pulled into his assigned space, and took the express elevator to the hundred and seventy-second floor. On the way up he smoothed down his hair, evened out his lapels, and pressed the off-button on his wristband transponder, just to be sure of no interruptions during this unusual Saturday meeting whose purpose he still didn't know. It was safe enough switching the transponder off temporarily since Byron was confined to his bedroom for the rest of the morning, where the odds of an emergency were relatively low.

With the wall clock in the Amalgamated MegaPhysics reception area striking nine a.m., Mr. Barnett stepped into the conference room and greeted his two bosses, Mr. Oleg Medley and Ms. Cindy de Hornet by name. Then, ever-so-slightly nervous, he sat down to find out why he was here.

Also at nine o'clock, back at the house, Mrs. Barnett was in the kitchen putting the finishing touches on a new recipe for oatmeal cookies. With the technique of a scientist she'd been experimenting all week long to find exactly the right proportions of coarse-cut oats, Vermont maple syrup, chewy currants, morsels of white chocolate, toasted macadamia nuts, secret spices, and creamy Dutch butter. She wore an apron over her ensemble of pink and cherry cashmere, to protect herself from puffs of flour and dabs of syrup; and she'd taken off her wedding band, her wristwatch, and her transponder so she could get her hands good and deep in the dough.

Just when she finished arranging a dozen gooey gobs on a baking tray and was about to pop the tray in the scanning electron oven, the power in the kitchen snapped off. Her hands sticky with ingredients, she elbowed the "Talk" button on the wall intercom and spoke into it:

"Byron, sweetheart, would you pop down to the atomic closet and flip the circuit breaker? The power's out in the kitchen, and I'm up to my elbows in cookie dough."

Back through the intercom came no answer from Byron, only the strains of Byron's violin.

"Byron?"

Still no answer.

Thinking Byron must be absorbed in his practicing, which would be a first and for that reason alone a mistake to interrupt, the lady of the house washed and dried her hands at the sink and went down to the basement, to the atomic closet, to deal with the circuits herself. Had she gone in the opposite direction, up through several glass polygons, past the second-floor den, up the third-floor staircase and into the Twelfth Deadly Realm (as Byron liked to call his room), she would've had a shock at what was missing there: Byron!

It was a battery-operated tape recorder that was pumping out the sounds of Byron playing the famous theme from Tchaikovsky's Violin Concerto in D Major, Opus 35, not a live performance by Byron in the flesh. Because Byron, at this very moment, was already a mile from home, racing on his mountain bike down the dirt road into the desert. José Ignacio was flying beside him under his own power, using his boot jets.

"Sneaking out of the house against orders is the conduct of a boy with a bleak future!" he warned Byron.

"Annoying the boy he shares a room with is the conduct of a robot who's gonna spend tomorrow in a broom closet!" Byron snapped back.

Arguing in this manner they advanced into the desert, whither Byron, on this of all Saturdays, was most specifically not supposed to go.

CHAPTER: 3

WAY OUT IN DEEP SPACE, that mighty white worm that we saw being born was now slurping in and glugging down everything in its vicinity, including a slew of meteoroids resulting from moons crashing into planets and planets crashing into moons, itself the by-product of the supernova whose implosion had produced the white worm in the first place.

If you were strapped to the top of one of those swallowed meteoroids, you'd right now be on the ride of your life, shooting as fast as a lightning bolt down a cosmic tunnel. Because the white worm's electrified rear had already zapped its way through quite a long stretch of space, creating what we call a "white wormhole," which is a shortcut straight through the universe! Where the meteoroids would end up—which is to say, where on the other side of the white wormhole the worm's supercharged anus (to use the technical term) would poop them out—was still unclear at this hour: an open question, a random riddle, an unknowable quirk of Creation ...

At the same time, on the blue orb of Earth, also moving at top speed was Byron Barnett, riding his mountain bike into the Arizona desert. He was still bickering with his robot, who flew beside him as they zipped past a lonely chlorophyll station that serviced the motor vehicles passing by on their way to the national park due east. The station attendant, a sombrero-wearing gentleman of a certain age, was just now filling a jeep's tank with deep green liquid. Holding the pump against the vehicle's intake funnel, he watched Byron race by on his bike, pedaling hard and yelling at a toy robot strapped by rubber band to the bike's handlebars. But from Byron's own

point of view, José Ignacio, fully seven feet and several centimeters tall, was in jet-powered flight alongside of him.

"Why can't you explore this cave on your own?" José
Ignacio shouted as they veered off the desert road toward the
canyons. "Do I really need to be here?"

"Dial it down, you insufferable semiconductor! We're
gonna take some measurements, collect a few rock samples,
and be back before lunch!"

"But why do we always have to drag ourselves so *far*?
Can't we just go home and fight monsters in the basement?"

"Boy versus Nature, José Ignacio! That's where the *real*
action is. Boy versus Monster is yesterday's news, cause your
average monster only has so many tricks up its sleeve, like
poison spit or flaming feces or foot-long talons to slice you
into a pile of spaghetti-flesh. If I've been sliced up once, I've
been sliced up a hundred times. Boy versus Boy is old hat
too, and I don't have any human adversaries anyway. Boy
versus Society is no fun, cause I *like* society. Boy versus Him-
self can be a challenge, except I'm on very good terms with
myself. But Nature? You *never* know what Nature's next
move is gonna be. Nature is a boy's best enemy!"

Back at the house, Mrs. Barnett—who still thought
Byron was up in his room practicing the violin—was now
the one in the basement, about to fight her own battle with,
if not exactly a monster, then a monstrous botheration. She
went into the atomic closet and flipped the circuit breaker
to turn the power back on in the kitchen. But the green light
next to the circuit in question did not come on, indicating
that the power in the kitchen had not been restored.

"Oh, for heaven's sake."

She bent down beside the safety-certified atomic generator, opened its access panel, and saw through a magnifying

square that the atom-splitter inside—a laser beam of the utmost precision—kept missing its atom. The generator was broken—again! With her husband downtown at Amalgamated MegaPhysics and Taji at City Center on his date, she would have to fix it herself. She opened the atomic closet's toolkit, swiveled her apron around so she could lie on her back without dirtying her skirt, and got down to business.

Byron was by this time ready to get down to business of his own in the desert. He and José Ignacio had entered the canyon and arrived at their destination: Devil's Drop Cave, a dark hole in a wall of red rock. Byron was now knotting and securing his climber's rope around a log of petrified wood while José Ignacio, still resisting the mission, complained:

"As the only person present with his wits about him—

"You're not a person," Byron interrupted.

"As the only 'entity' present with his wits about him, I feel compelled to state for the record how deeply dangerous this is."

"I laugh at danger!" Byron said. "I spit in danger's face!" He hocked up a glob and spat into the cave to illustrate his point.

"Which is it? You laugh or you spit?"

"I laugh *then* I spit. Then I be*friend* danger! I invite danger in for a slice of pizza! I tell danger my life story and danger loves listening!"

"You're both a disturbed and a disturbing individual."

"I'm an explorer! Some day they're gonna *name* things after me!"

"Yes, personality disorders."

"Just start recording what we see on your memory bulb."

José Ignacio triggered an internal switch, causing the memory bulb in his transparent cranium to begin flickering.

Byron fastened the climber's rope around his belt and worked it through two hooks on José Ignacio's metallic waist. Together they entered the dark mouth of the cave, Byron shining his flashlight from side to side.

"It's empty," José Ignacio said. "Let's go home."

"Keep moving!"

They came to the edge of a surprisingly wide hole in the cave floor, at least twenty feet across.

"Zanzibar!" whispered Byron. (Yes, Zanzibar is a group of islands off the coast of East Africa, but it was also Byron's personal word for expressing emotions of the amazed variety.)

With satisfaction, he turned to José Ignacio and announced:

"I give you 'Devil's Drop.'"

"You want to go down *this*? It's bottomless!"

"And that's why it's gonna be *good!*"

A debate followed, but José Ignacio failed to stamp out Byron's enthusiasm. So over the robot's strongly worded objections, he and Byron were soon lowering themselves by rope down this most awesome of all local holes.

"You see?" Byron said, "it's safe as a—

The log of petrified wood outside the cave's entrance gave way—the log to which Byron's climber's rope was attached—sending Byron and José Ignacio plummeting. In free fall, boy and robot shrieked at the top of their lungs, or in José Ignacio's case at the top of his audio-generator—until their rope snapped taut again, leaving them dangling but unharmed.

The sudden, mid-air stop knocked the wind out of Byron all the same; he needed a minute to compose himself with some deep breathing. What he should've guessed but was still too shaken to calculate was that although the log had gotten caught at the cave's entrance up above, saving them, the danger had not yet passed. The knot holding the rope around its anchor of petrified wood had come loose when it hit the mouth of the cave. Now it came apart.

Byron and José Ignacio shrieked again as they plummeted a second time ... but both the shrieking and the plummeting were brief, since the remaining drop to the ground was only three feet and an inch or two: enough to bruise but not wound.

Byron stood up, dusted himself off, switched his flashlight back on, and craned his neck to look up just as the other end of the rope came falling down—and slapped José Ignacio full on the face, or full on the front of the glass cranium, to be accurate about it.

"You call that securing a *rope?*" the robot demanded.

"Let's not play the blame game," Byron said. Then, glancing around, his eyes lit up. "Stalactites!" he said.

"How very thrilling," said José Ignacio.

"Did you know that stalactites come from the minerals in dripping water? From the same stuff *egg*shells are made of!"

"May I just say, this whole situation confirms what I've long believed and often pointed out about you."

"Namely?"

"That you're no boy-genius! My central processing unit has *twice* the raw computing power of the lump of jelly you call your brain! And holds ten times as much information!"

"And yet, José Ignacio, here we both are, in the same boat—together."

"Exactly! Because of *you!*"

"Land o'Goshen! Could you please—for once—stop *moan*ing! This is just a temporary setback!"

"And why do you say *that?*"

"Because unlike you, you condescending calculator, I know that information is only the *second* best thing you can have in your head."

"The first best being?"

"*Imag*ination!"

"I see. And how exactly is your 'imagination' going to get us out of here?"

"Well, let me jiggle my 'brain jelly' for a minute and I'll come back to you on that."

Byron was of course being sarcastic about his brain jelly, but José Ignacio was unamused. A robot has no eyes, or else he would've rolled them to express how very unamused he actually was. Meanwhile, Byron was randomly moving his head left and right, up and down, diagonally and semi-circularly, to jiggle, joggle, and otherwise agitate his gray matter until his imagination kicked in.

"Okay!" he said suddenly, "I've got it!" He reached down to his belt buckle (which was the size of a tin of mints), slid open its top to get into its secret compartment, and took out a red ball of something the shape and color of a maraschino cherry. "I could detonate my gob of emergency plasma!" he said. "It'll blow open a dimensional portal that we could jump through. I don't know which of the eleven deadly realms we'd end *up* in, but at least we'd be out of *here*."

"Why do you even *have* emergency plasma? You know it's unstable!"

José Ignacio wasn't wrong: emergency plasma was a dangerous substance to be carrying around in a secret compartment in your belt buckle: if it detonated by accident, it could blow off your belly button and set your intestines on fire. (And FYI: the cherry bomb that this emergency plasma in real life really was, was almost as risky.)

"Listen, you aggravating automaton," Byron said, "do you want me to try it or not?"

"Not."

"So you're saying you'd rather stay stuck here?"

"Knowing you, if you try to light that gob, it'll go off before you fling it, and I'm reasonably certain your mother would appreciate you showing up at the dinner table tonight with all your fingers still attached to your hands."

"Okay ... well, you *could* just fly up, re-attach the rope, and pull me out."

"My boot jets cracked in the fall, thank you very much. I can't fly."

He showed off the cracks in both his heels. Byron said:

"Then maybe I can use my grappling hook to get us far enough up to climb the rest of the way." He attached the fallen rope to a small grappling hook that he carried on his belt during spelunking scenarios, then flung it up, managing to catch it around one of a hundred rocky spikes above. Pleased with himself, he glanced at José Ignacio and gloated:

"On the first try."

He yanked hard on the rope—and the entire shelf of foot-long stalactites came plunging down. Shrieking for the third time in as many minutes, Byron and José Ignacio dropped to the ground and lay flat on their backs, where they were pinned into position by the shelf of downward-pointing rocky daggers. By pure luck none of the stalactites had pierced Byron's body, but he was now completely trapped: sandwiched between the floor of the cave and the rock shelf resting a mere foot off the ground, immobilized by dozens of stalactites, some of them pinning his clothes into the ground, others only a hair's breadth from his face.

"Brilliant," said José Ignacio. "What now?"

"I'm not quite sure. Any ideas?"

"As a matter of fact, yes. You're going to have to use your transponder."

The mere mention of this sent chills up Byron's spine. "I can't do *that*!" he said. "My parents will find out we're here! It won't be a pretty picture!"

"*You* won't be pretty picture when you turn into a skeleton in this cave! Use the transponder!"

Byron gnawed beaver-like at his lip, then bit halfway down his chin. He felt rather abnormally stressed. Using the transponder would most probably save his skin, but using the transponder would also alert his parents to the slight gap between being in his room practicing the violin and lying at the bottom of Devil's Drop Cave facing a substantially reduced life expectancy.

There was already a certain question in the Barnett household about Byron's general "veracity"—which was his parents' word for telling the truth. What they didn't seem to understand was that getting *to* the truth was like chasing a butterfly, not like following a laser beam. Nevertheless, letting his parents know that he was trapped underground in the desert without permission, or that he was out of the house at all, would, Byron feared, be seen by them as an admission of guilt on his part, proof that he lacked exactly the kind of veracity they'd been putting such an emphasis on lately.

"Use—the—trans*ponder*!" José Ignacio said.

"No! There has to be another way!"

"Give it to me!" The robot was no less boxed in by stalactites than Byron, but his metallic arm was long and sufficiently hinged to reach over and pinch his carbon-based companion. With Byron screaming bloody murder, José Ignacio managed to get a claw around Byron's wrist, flicked open the crystal face on Byron's transponder, and pushed its panic button.

Ultrasonic waves began emanating from the device: they shot up and out the cave, spread across the desert, and reached as far as Arizona City in a matter of seconds. In the soda shop at City Center, Taji's own transponder, picking up Byron's emergency signal, started flashing its warning. But in the semi-privacy of a corner booth, Taji and his date were busy "osculating," which was the word that Arizonan teens were using at the time to mean kissing. With his arms around her shoulders, his lips pressing pleasantly against hers, and his eyes understandably closed, Taji did not see his transponder light up.

Nor did Mr. Barnett, in the Amalgamated MegaPhysics tower a few blocks away, see *his*. He was sitting alone now in the conference room, in a state of shock from the meeting with his bosses that had recently wrapped up. His transponder—which he'd turned off before his meeting, to avoid interruptions—was dark. Even Mrs. Barnett didn't see her transponder flashing. It sat on the kitchen counter, beside her wedding band and wristwatch, while Mrs. Barnett herself was down in the basement, in the atomic closet, lying on her back working on the generator, the way a mechanic works beneath a car, an open toolkit beside her.

At the bottom of Devil's Drop Cave, Byron started to worry. Apropos his transponder, he told José Ignacio:

"It's supposed to blink green when they signal back they're on their way."

"I see neither blinking nor green."

"Maybe it doesn't work this far down."

"So you've got us trapped in a stalactite prison a hundred feet underground with no one knowing we're here and no possibility of rescue. Not how I was hoping to spend my Saturday."

Back at the house, Mrs. Barnett only needed another minute to finish her repairs on the generator and restore the power flow. Once this was done, she packed away the toolkit, sealed up the atomic closet, went upstairs, and stepped into the kitchen—where she spotted her transponder flashing on the kitchen counter.

Snatching it up, she quickly took the back staircase to the third floor, where she found Byron's bedroom Byron-less and the sound of his violin coming from a tape recorder. Without missing a beat, she pressed the locator-button on her transponder, causing a holographic map to be projected from the device, including a blinking dot showing Byron's whereabouts.

Next she raced back downstairs, hurried into the garage, and ripped the emergency flight-pack from its locker. A moment later she came running outside, throwing off her apron and strapping the flight-pack on tight. She took hold of its joystick, blasted up into the sky, swiveled toward open desert, and shot off in the direction of her son's signal.

At about the same time, at Amalgamated MegaPhysics, Mr. Barnett switched his transponder back on while exiting the express elevator into the underground parking structure. The device instantly started flashing—and Mr. Barnett's face went white. He ran for his vehicle, dove in, and peeled out, the bubble-topped sedan squealing with speed as it shot up the ramp and out the building.

At the soda shop a few blocks away, Taji was still osculating with his girlfriend of the moment when he opened his eyes and saw her ear flashing on and off. He pulled his hand out from behind her neck, confirming that the transponder around his wrist was the source of the radiance. He jumped up from the booth, made a quick apology, ran outside, and spotted a policeman biting into a fruit tartlet beside his parked hovership.

At the bottom of Devil's Drop Cave, Byron's transponder started blinking green, indicating that someone in his family had received his distress signal and was heading his way to help.

"Satisfied?" he asked José Ignacio.

And that's when something crackled overhead. Not the pleasant kind of crackle you get in your cereal bowl after pouring milk on rice crispies, this was more a horrifying kind of crackle, like the sound your bones make when an ogre has you between his teeth and he's snacking on you, on your hip bone and your collarbone and one or both of your fibulas, plus a couple of ribs and maybe even your skull.

Managing to wiggle his official Astral Corps multi-tool out of his pants pocket (because remember: Byron was flat on his back and trapped underneath a shelf of rock just a few inches above his face), he opened the tool's medium blade, jabbed it up, hit a thin bit of rock, and poked through. After aiming his flashlight into the little hole he'd made, he saw that the fallen shelf of stalactites pinning him down had revealed on the roof of the cave a *second* rock-shelf, now cracking around the edges and threatening to come down, this one bearing clearly deadly five-foot-long stalactites. Even Byron couldn't spit in danger's face *this* time.

Fortunately, Mrs. Barnett, Mr. Barnett, and Taji were already converging on Byron's coordinates, coming in from three different directions: Mrs. Barnett via flight-pack, Mr. Barnett in his sedan, Taji in a police hovership. Once there, the three police officers that Taji rode in with quickly set up their rescue equipment outside the cave while Mrs. Barnett familiarized herself with their electro-dynamic vocal-cone. She switched it to maximum, borrowed her husband's handkerchief to wipe off her lipstick, put her mouth to the vocal-cone's mouthpiece, and called into the cave, her voice dramatically amplified:

"BYRON! CAN YOU HEAR ME?!"

Up from the depths of Devil's Drop echoed Byron's faraway reply:

"YOU DIDN'T HAVE TO COME ALL THE WAY OUT HERE, MOM! I'M FINE!"

The ludicrousness of this statement was made plain as the ranking police officer on the scene, Officer Matsumoto by name, aimed a snooperscope into the cave. He turned a knob to expand its beam and reach the cave's floor, revealing on its screen a visual of Byron—and Byron's toy robot—pinned to the ground by a shelf of stalactites, with another shelf of five-foot stalactites cracking apart above and ready to plunge.

Mr. Barnett took the vocal-cone from his wife and spoke into it:

"BYRON, JUST HOLD STILL, WE'RE GOING TO GET YOU OUT OF THERE!"

"NO RUSH! TAKE YOUR TIME!"

From his trapped position down below, Byron could not see that two of the police officers had hurried into the cave, aimed their rope-rifles down the hole, and fired titanium-tipped cords into the bottom shelf of stalactites. They were now hurrying back out of the cave holding the loose ends of the cords—but at this exact moment the top shelf of stalactites snapped, and Byron let out an ear-splitting scream as the five-foot spikes plunged at him ...

... which is when the police hovership lifted off outside, Officer Matsumoto at the controls. The ship pulled the bottom rock-shelf up with it—since Officer Matsumoto's colleagues had swiftly hooked their cords to the hovership's underside. The rising, bottom shelf of stalactites caught the dropping *top* shelf of stalactites—and Byron was saved. Watching the spikes reverse course and fly up and away from him, he felt the scream rocketing out of his lungs morph into a crazy giggle.

Soon Byron too was hoisted by rope out of the cave, courtesy of all three policemen. His parents stood watching with a mixture of distress and relief as he emerged from the shadows still giggling, his toy robot dangling by rubber band from his belt. His giggling ceased on the spot when he noticed that nobody else looked amused.

"I can explain almost everything," he said.

With Mr. Barnett thanking the police officers beside their hovership, Byron sat between his mother and brother in the back seat of the family sedan, its bubble-top opened for air circulation, since it was almost eleven o'clock and the desert was heating up. Mrs. Barnett was holding a water bottle for Byron to sip from, through a straw.

"No more cliffs, no more caverns, no more caves," she warned. "Do we understand each other?"

Byron nodded.

"Say it," Mrs. Barnett insisted.

"No more cliffs, no more caverns, no more caves."

"*Especially* caves. No—more—spelunking."

Just now Mr. Barnett stepped away from the police officers to join his family. He looked down at Byron and shook his head.

"Byron Barnett, your judgment here was appalling and your behavior a scandal. But we're going to have to discuss what's happened in detail at a later time—because believe it or not, today's headline belongs to *me*. So if no one minds, I'd like to get right to it."

Not only did no one mind, but everyone was gripped by an intense curiosity to hear more.

"They didn't fire me at the office," Mr. Barnett continued, "in fact they did the opposite: they promoted me. With a transfer. To the engineering department ... of the Lunar League. Bianca Barnett, Brothers Barnett—how would you like to move to the Moon?"

Mouths fell open, but no one spoke, they were all too stunned. The group silence—a rare occurrence in the Barnett family—lasted six or seven seconds, after which Taji asked:

"There are *girls* on the Moon, right?"

"Yes, Romeo. There are girls on the Moon."

"A man has to have his priorities, Pops."

Mr. Barnett turned to Byron for his thoughts; but Byron was in a trance: eyes wide, teeth showing, his mind already a quarter million miles away. So Mr. Barnett turned to the person whose opinion mattered the most.

"Love of my life? What's your feeling about it?"

"Well, it's an enormous decision," Mrs. Barnett said.

"It *would* mean a big raise in salary. If we hate it, we can always come home after two years. But I only said we'd consider it."

"I don't know, Wallace. Taji has to start visiting colleges next summer. I'd miss the flower show this October: that means three years of work in the garden gone to waste. And your youngest son is a disaster-magnet right here on Planet Earth. How many more disasters are waiting for him out in space?"

"Or … looking at it another way: in lunar gravity he could fall off a cliff, land on his head, and barely put a dent in his skull. The Moon might be the safest place *for* him. But if you say nay, we won't go."

"What?!" Byron said, snapping out of his trance. "Why does *mom* get to decide?"

"Because she's the brains of this operation!"

Byron bit his tongue, then focused his most significant expression on his mother. In a low voice he implored her:

"Mommy, I'm begging you. After all these years, my life finally makes sense! I'll *die* if I don't move to the Moon. I'll absolutely keel over and expire! Living on the Moon is what I was *born* for! It's the answer to my every riddle and the solution to my every problem! It's my future! It's my fate! It's my personal destiny!"

Mrs. Barnett looked in no way won over.

"I do hear the Moon is quite the romantic milieu for persons of the adult persuasion," Mr. Barnett said.

Mrs. Barnett seemed truly sorry to be the voice of reason; nevertheless she had to speak honestly. "I don't think it's in the best interests of this family to leave terra firma," she explained. "I understand how exciting the Moon sounds from a distance, but I won't apologize for wanting us to stay happy, healthy, and safe right here in an oxygen-rich environment."

It was now that Officer Matsumoto, who for the past several minutes had been talking on the police radio in his hovership, came over to have a last word with the Barnetts.

"Byron, don't you have something you'd like to say to Officer Matsumoto?" Mrs. Barnett prompted.

"Thank you very much, Officer Matsumoto, for saving me from being skewered by stalactites. I really appreciate it."

"You're welcome, Byron. Unfortunately, you're also under arrest."

CHAPTER: 4

THE CITY COURTHOUSE WAS BUILT entirely of intersecting slabs of glass, coincidentally out of the same school of architecture as the Barnetts' own house of glass polygons, though many times larger. In Courtroom 2-Q, the Barnetts sat quietly in the front row, the rest of the high-ceilinged, sun-blasted chamber empty behind them.

On the glass platform in front of them was Judge Arthur T. Monday, an eighty-year-old elder of the Navajo Nation as well as a respected member of the Arizona Bar. He was reading Byron's case file. When he finished, he looked up and addressed the defendant directly:

"Byron Barnett, it seems you're in violation of Municipal Ordinance 1441: excessive use of emergency and/or utility services. The city's police and fire departments, as well as the power company, the water company, and for reasons I don't fully understand from these notes the sewage company, have been called out a total of six times on your behalf in the last fifteen months, in each case for an emergency of your own making. How do you plead?"

Byron raised his hand and said:

"Present."

"You're guilty!" whispered José Ignacio into Byron's ear. "Guilty like a bowl of burnt ravioli!"

"I'm afraid, Byron," said Judge Monday, "that 'present' is not a valid plea."

Byron turned to his father, who, reminding him what they'd discussed on the ride to the courthouse, whispered:

"No con—

"Right!" Byron blurted, turning back toward the judge. "No contest! I plead no contest!"

Byron looked pleased with himself, as if he'd just remembered the quadratic formula during a pop quiz; but Judge Monday was unimpressed. "Young man," he said, "you do understand what 'no contest' means, do you not?"

"It means you win without having to beat me! It's like you get to legally cheat!"

Mrs. Barnett chirped in alarm, even though she knew Byron's definition was not all wrong.

Judge Monday stared at Byron for a long, hard moment before replying: "How is it cheating when I have a record of your overuse of emergency services in my hand? Is it your position that the six incidents listed here were not, in fact, all your fault?"

"I mean, I was there when they all *happened*," Byron said.

Mr. Barnett put his hand over his eyes and shook his head.

"I'd like to be very clear about this," the judge told Byron. "Are you denying to the court that you have a long habit of making large mistakes?"

"Let me ask *this*," Byron countered. "Have you ever heard the old adage: When you make a mistake, never say 'Oops!' Always say 'Ah, *interesting*!' "

Judge Monday turned to Mrs. Barnett and stated flatly:

"I'd thought this was a basic mischief situation we were dealing with, but now I'm wondering: do we have a serious dishonesty problem going on here? We're in a court of law, where I'm sure I don't need to remind you that the requirement of truthfulness is absolute."

"Oh, no, no, no, Your Honor," Mrs. Barnett promised. "We may have a slight exaggeration tendency that we've been addressing, but Byron was certainly *not* raised to be untruthful, I can give you my personal assurance of that."

"The judge thinks you're a liar!" José Ignacio whispered to Byron.

Byron nudged the robot's titanium torso, to shut him up. But José Ignacio persisted:

"Look at your parents! They're mortified. Because of *you*."

Mr. Barnett cleared his throat and asked for the court's indulgence, confirming for the record that Byron's plea of "no contest" had been accurate and offered with the utmost respect.

Looking irked, Judge Monday picked up his pen and wrote Byron's plea into the case file, saying:

"I suppose we can move along then to the penalty portion of these proceedings. You have several options. I can fine you 75,000 credits as reimbursement for the use of city services. If you're unable to pay at the present time, we can garnish your future earnings." He thumbed the buttons on his adding machine while mumbling: "Let's say you hold off making payment until you're twenty-five years of age: with interest the grand total will come to ... 998,352 credits."

"A million credits?!" whispered Mrs. Barnett to her husband. "He'll be crushed by debt!"

"We could pay the 75,000 right now and be done with it," Mr. Barnett whispered back.

"But that would wipe out the boys' college fund!"

Mrs. Barnett turned to ask the judge: "You mentioned options, Your Honor?"

"Yes. In lieu of a cash fine, I could sentence Byron to a hundred hours of community service."

"I don't suppose a hundred extra hours of violin lessons would count," Mrs. Barnett said. "Or sending him to an after-school tutor to improve his Spanish? His accent truly needs work; his own grandparents can barely understand him when they visit from Bogotá. He can't trill his r's—at *all*."

Byron grimaced at the mental picture of so heinous a penalty being imposed upon him as extra violin lessons or after-school schooling; but Judge Monday was imagining an altogether different kind of punishment:

"I'm thinking something more along the lines of poop-duty at the zoo."

José Ignacio was thrilled. "A hundred hours of shoveling elephant dung?" he whispered to Byron. "I *love* this judge!"

Mrs. Barnett, however, was horrified. She whispered to Mr. Barnett:

"I'm not shipping our child off to hard labor in a zoo!"

"Your Honor," said Mr. Barnett in his most courteous tone, "I wonder if there's anything else you could propose. Anything at all."

"Well, for adult offenders we sometimes allow corrective exile. But I'd consider it in this case, if you prefer."

"I'm sorry, 'corrective exile?' "

"Byron would be required to vacate the jurisdiction for a period of not less than two years. He'd have to leave the state."

"Leave the state?" asked Mrs. Barnett in alarm. "We can't send our nine-year-old son out of Arizona by himself for two years."

"You could always go *with* him."

"Go *with* him? Go with him *where*?"

A tiny smile worked its way across Byron's lips as he turned to José Ignacio and peered through the robot's cranium of safety glass to the tubes, magnets, switches, and resistors within. José Ignacio, for his part, had no trouble deducing what was going on inside *Byron's* brain, where synapses were firing manically and neurotransmitters were bursting in chemical glee with the realization that Judge Monday had just made possible Byron's move to the Moon, after all.

Three weeks later, their house rented as of the following morning and their luggage already sent ahead, Byron was in his room dressing for departure when José Ignacio started complaining about the hinge on his lower back panel, which was popping open again but which he had trouble reaching on his own.

"I'll get my toolkit," Byron said.

He stepped into the closet and came out kit in hand to find that José Ignacio had seated himself at their card table and rotated his titanium corpus so that Byron could more easily operate on the pesky panel. Byron went to work while José Ignacio sat facing the laminated poster of the Moon that filled the wall between the card table and the window, a poster eight-feet-tall by eight-feet-wide. The *really* interesting thing about the poster, however, wasn't its size, but its palette. This was no silver-gray Moon like the one we normally see in the night sky; it was, instead, a high-resolution lunar photograph to which a medley of colors had been applied, from fluorescent strawberry to unusually bold purple to daffodil yellow, pistachio green, popsicle blue, and vivid tangerine. How Byron had come to own such a dazzling item is worth a brief detour to explain …

Three months earlier, Taji Barnett had given up his Saturday afternoon to drive Byron to—and spend several hours wandering around with him *at*—ZipperCon, the big science and technology exposition held every spring at the Arizona Convention Center. Sponsoring the event this year was Amalgamated MegaPhysics—a giant in the science biz and, of course, the very company that Byron's father worked for—so the Barnett boys had free tickets. Mr. Barnett had been called out to California the day before to handle an engineering emergency at the flight-pack factory in San Diego that Amalgamated MegaPhysics had designed, but before leaving had asked Taji to fill in as Byron's chauffeur and chaperone.

No science nut, Taji had figured he could live through a few hours at an eggheads' convention by introducing himself to a new group of girls than he normally mixed with. Byron himself had very different plans. As the brothers strolled the booths together, Taji admired the young ladies while Byron gawked at the gizmos. Hundreds of apparatuses, innovations, and iterations cried out for his scrutiny. His favorites were a laser-backscratcher; a two-inch-tornado maker; a bionic tongue; and a "dream-pistol" whose sonic bullet caused a fleeing criminal to drop into a calming nap (—Byron volunteered to be the criminal in a demonstration, but the man in the booth directed him to a display screen to watch a pre-recorded demonstration instead).

His second favorites were a fingernail flashlight; a wristwatch Geiger counter; a vitamin that let you see through walls for an hour at a time; and a one-dog submarine. What a treasure trove! Unfortunately none of these devices and only a few of the doodads were actually for sale. Except at the booth for Hawaii's Kumaka-poipoi Observatory. Here any number of photographs of the cosmos could be snapped up for the price of a pack of gum. Neutron stars ... asteroid belts ... rogue planets ... blue supergiants ... hot Neptunes ...

globular clusters ... galactic bulges: the telescopes at
Kumaka-poipoi had captured everything excellent about
outer space.

Byron was now seriously contemplating the purchase of
an eight-by-twelve-inch glossy of the Crab Nebula when he
looked over and noticed tacked to a rolling corkboard the
previously mentioned eight-foot-by-eight-foot laminated
poster of the Moon in all its multicolored glory. The astrophysicist manning the booth saw him eying the poster and
stepped over to discuss it (even though she was a lady—so
was she "womaning" the booth Byron wondered?).

"It's a false-color photo," she said.

"I'm unfamiliar with the term," Byron admitted.

"It's when we add our own colors to a photograph to better
see what's there. For example, false colors help the eye perceive
differences in elevation in a topographical picture—what's
higher up or lower down: mountains might be magenta while
valleys would be baby blue—or differences in temperature if
we're looking at a thermal imaging map, what's hotter versus
what's colder ... or in a satellite picture of a landmass, false
colors would make it easier to see where the vegetation is compared to the soil: the plants could be orange and the ground
could be lavender. Without false colors, or sometimes we call
them 'pseudo colors,' all the black-and-white data in a picture
can blend together, making it harder to know what you're
looking at."

"So on *this* poster," Byron said, "the colors are there to
make the craters and stuff pop out? So you notice them?"

"You got it. Otherwise your eye just glides over the
Moon's silver-gray and you miss things. But with these false
colors added in, presto! Everything that's there shows up for
you."

"I'll take it!" Byron said. Reaching into his pocket for his credit-key, he asked, after-the-fact: "How much?"

"Let me check on that," the lady said, stepping over to the poster and plucking a thumb tack from the top corner so she could find the price on back. "That'll be … a hundred and twenty credits."

Byron turned to Taji and grinned hopefully.

"You're joking," Taji said. "You want me to lend you a hundred and twenty credits?!"

"You have the money from your job!"

This was true: Taji had saved up quite a tidy sum from his after-school job as an artist's assistant. The artist in question, Mr. Hafez le Bone, was a portrait-painter who combined old-school photography with up-to-the-minute computer graphics to turn out beautifully unique images of his subjects. His business used to be mostly in baby pictures and wedding portraits, but since Taji started working for him, teenage girls had been coming into the studio in droves to be "painted." They seemed to love Taji fussing over their clothes and getting the lighting on their cheeks just right for the camera. Business was now so good thanks to Taji that Mr. le Bone was paying him three times the normal assistant's salary, just to keep him around. But Taji hadn't been working so hard for his health.

"Boon, you *know* I'm saving up for a hoverpod."

"Please! It won't slow you down *that* much. We can make it an early birthday present! I'm sure you were planning on getting me something big for my tenth!"

"Not *this* big."

"Then I'll pay you back!"

"How? Your allowance is five credits a week. It'll take you half a *year* to pay me back. And that's *if* you go half a year without spending any allowance at all! Are you saying you'll last six months without candy or comics? Or are you going to stop buying your pigment pills and go back to all black?"

"I do like the royal blue," the lady in the booth said.

She meant Byron's hair. Which, again, was *cobalt* blue. Why people didn't know the differences between colors Byron could never figure out—especially a person who'd just explained how she added colors to the Moon! It was actually extremely irritating. A lot of the time Byron would have to inform mistake-makers that cobalt blue was different from royal blue just like sky blue was different from robin's-egg blue and baby blue was different from cornflower blue, not to mention the differences between all the blues that didn't even have "blue" in their names: cerulean, indigo, cyan, viridian, teal, ultramarine, and so forth. But since he was considering asking the lady in the booth for a student discount on the poster he wanted to buy off her, he decided not to correct her on her color-related ignorance in this instance. Instead he turned back to his brother and said:

"Okay, okay! I *won't* pay you back! At least not in the instantaneous future! But further down the road, in the *long* run, someway, someday, somehow, I'll do *something* that'll make it worth your while to buy this for me right *now*! Please!!"

Byron grinned again—he seemed to think this was one of his most charming expressions, though really it made him look like a crazy monkey baring its teeth. Taji only groaned. Nevertheless, the truth was, Taji hated turning Byron down. When a sibling asks for help, saying no is just plain rude. Taji reached into his pocket for his credit-key, slotted it into the Kumaka-poipoi booth's debit box, turned to Byron and informed him:

"This is your birthday present from me for the next five years."

Byron clapped his hands in glee and gave Taji a hearty handshake of thanks. Then he dashed into the booth to help the lady roll up his poster and pack it into a protective tube. It was a shame, he thought, that he'd left José Ignacio at home today, since the poster tube was twice Byron's height and the robot could've toted it with ease. But ZipperCon was almost over anyway, so it wouldn't be too much toting.

Three months later, back in Byron's bedroom on the day the Barnetts were leaving Arizona to live on the Moon itself, José Ignacio was still staring at the colorized poster while Byron continued fiddling at the robot's back panel. After several minutes José Ignacio said:

"You're not fixing me with paper clips, are you?"

"Don't be abzurd. I'm using a titanium clamp and four of the micro-hinges you insisted I send away for, at three credits apiece, by the way."

"Exactly my point. Those hinges aren't cheap. How do I know you didn't use up your allowance on Turkish Taffy and you're repairing me with office supplies out of your mother's desk drawer? You *say* you're using a titanium clamp and micro-hinges that you sent away for, but your record for telling the truth is very much in question these days."

"Listen, you preposterous mechanism, do you want me to fix you or not?!"

"Fine. Just get it over with. I don't like your sticky fingers in my framework this long."

"Then stop talking and let me finish!"

But José Ignacio could only keep quiet for a moment. Apropos the eight-foot-by-eight-foot poster of the Moon filling the wall in front of him, he commented skeptically:

"I still don't know about this acquisition of yours. If I'd been with you at ZipperCon, I would've tried talking you out of buying it. For starters, it looks nothing like the real Moon. It looks like somebody's hallucination of a moon made out of a jar of jelly beans."

"I've told you four hundred and twenty-six times, it's not *supposed* to look like the real Moon. They add the colors to make the craters and such stand *out*. That's why they're called 'false' colors or 'pseudo' colors. It's very scientific! The point is to help you see what's there *differently*, not the same way you always do! So you can see things *better*. For instance, without all the colors added in, I'd never have spotted Rattlesnake Rill!"

A "rill" was a groove in the surface of the Moon, a naturally-formed channel of which there were hundreds if not thousands. Byron had discovered this particular rill, which looked to him like a rattler slithering along, while inspecting the prized poster through a magnifying glass. He'd named the rill himself after failing to find it in his Space Encyclopedia, which included a Moon map of its own alongside an alphabetical list of every already-named lunar feature. In fact Rattlesnake Rill was so small compared to the canyon it sat in that the only reason Byron had noticed it in the first place was because his poster of the Moon was so huge—and because, as he'd said, the snaky groove in the lunar surface was highlighted by a patch of false-color cotton-candy pink that drew the examining eye right to it.

"Aren't 'false' and 'pseudo' just different words for 'lies'?" José Ignacio said.

This aggravated Byron intensely, as at least half José Ignacio's questions usually did. He opened his mouth to set the robot straight, but the intercom on his night table chimed at the same time and Mrs. Barnett's voice came through:

"Byron, you've packed too many snacks. Come down and put half of these back in the pantry. The renters have three boys who I'm sure will appreciate some of your treats when they get here."

Byron jumped to the night table and jabbed the intercom's "Talk" button:

"I can't put back *half*! I'll starve!"

"You do not need chocolate-covered pretzels AND pretzel rods with chocolate filling. They're the same thing."

"I could not disagree with you more!"

"Byron, this is a forty-minute car ride, not a polar expedition. Now go use the bathroom, come downstairs, and choose ONE snack to take with you! We're leaving here in fifteen minutes."

Fifteen minutes later the family sedan pulled out of the garage and started down the street, but stopped short at the corner mailbox. Here the right rear passenger door popped open and Byron hopped out.

He quickly started pushing twenty-five postcards through the mailbox slot, five at a time. These were his official change-of-address notifications, stamped and ready to go to friends and acquaintances as well as the circulation departments at the several magazines he subscribed to. Also, and most crucially, one was going to Mr. Berkenbosch at the comic book store. Byron had already called Mr. Berkenbosch to explain the situation directly, but he wanted to be doubly sure that the standing order for his eight favorite comics would be sent to him once a month at his new address, the address he'd written with more than a little satisfaction and as neatly as possible in green magic marker on every card:

Byron Barnett
The Moon
Space.

After pushing the last batch through the slot, Byron hopped back in the car. Three minutes later the Barnetts were zipping down the Arizona hyper-highway, heading for the Southwestern Spaceport. Mr. Barnett was driving, Mrs. Barnett was in the front passenger seat writing a letter to her sister. In back, Taji was reading the latest issue of *Car & Hovercraft*, while Byron sat with earphones on, watching a documentary on the back-seat telescreen. He'd insisted that José Ignacio put on a pair of earphones and watch too, so they were now both engrossed in *The Story Of The Moon*.

With its bright, black-and-white footage and spellbinding voiceover, the film told the tale of their extraterrestrial destination. The narrator was that famous actor Alexander Fanta, he of the movies about the mutant panda bears who in the future fight the human race for control of the Earth. A brilliant choice, Byron thought. Mr. Fanta's voice thrilled and edified in equal measure as he explained:

> ... it was only with the discovery of diamonds on the Moon that lunar colonization finally took off. The next several years were much like the California Goldrush: gung-ho and lawless. Hundreds of prospectors landed in private rocket-ships, armed with little more than dreams and drills.
>
> With no governing body to organize them, these fortune-seekers built their dwellings willy-nilly beneath the lunar surface and began sifting through the regolith— which is the Moon's soft top layer—looking for gem-stones. Some struck it rich, amassing fortunes from the blue-white diamonds they found, none more so than J. Marcus Mingus, aka "Moonbeard Marc," one of the great adventurer-eccentrics of the era, who found such a

number of precious stones that he famously braided them into his hair and beard, just because he could.

According to legend, Moonbeard Marc spent the bulk of his wealth building himself a secret lunar palace somewhere underground, then one day vanished into it and was never seen again. But every year for seven years thereafter, on Moonbeard Marc's birthday, fireworks appeared in the lunar sky to the delight of all Moon-dwellers.

No one could ever track down where they came from, and though the connection to Moonbeard Marc could not be proven, back on Earth he'd spent a decade working as a chemist at a pyrotechnics firm in Tornado, Texas. So he certainly had the know-how to build specialized fireworks that would work in the vacuum of space.

Yet many of his fellow prospectors on the Moon were less successful in their efforts. Ill-equipped for the difficulties of lunar life without the support of a government, they resorted to bad behavior: stealing precious supplies of oxygen and foodstuffs from their neighbors and turning the Moon into a wild and sometimes wicked locale.

It took the creation of the Lunar League, backed by the great nations of the Earth, to establish order, harmony, and prosperity for all. Today the Moon is a paragon of peaceful cooperation: an autonomous Earth colony administered by an elected governor and home to some five thousand colonists, including miners, scientists, doctors, homemakers, schoolchildren, artists, and poets: a truly beautiful human foothold in space.

Here the little film came to an end. Byron turned away from the telescreen and glanced out the window at the giant cactuses lining the sides of the hyper-highway: fifty feet tall and crowned with white flowers.

Then the sedan followed a curve in the roadway, and something up ahead caused a grin to break across Byron's face: they were in sight of the Southwestern Spaceport, where a row of rocket-ships stood against the afternoon sky. As they sped closer, Byron's eye came upon what he considered to be the single-greatest sight that he'd beheld in all his nine years and eleven months: a shiny red rocket-ship lying horizontally on a metal scaffold, where it was being powered up for flight: a beauteous craft of chrome, curves, and fins: a rocket-ship that would lift him to his destiny, its name enameled elegantly on one of its fins: a rocket-ship called *The Biarritz*.

CHAPTER: 5

SUDDENLY IT WAS CLEAR where those meteoroids were whizzing. Not the meteoroids that Byron had dodged in his imagination while retrieving his mother's cape from the flagpole over his lunar fort, but the real ones, from the aftermath of that supernova way out in the cosmic deep. Racing along their cosmic shortcut, through their white wormhole, from one end of a white worm to the other, *those* meteoroids were headed … toward *us*!

The worm's rear end, when it finished zapping its way through the folds and fabric of space, was going to end up in our own solar system, where its supercharged anus would expel a flood of space-rocks. What's worse, on the worm's front end, where it was still yanking in objects with its rays of gravitation, an outlying moon was beginning to give way to the pull. Once the moon whizzed through the worm's wormy body and shot out the other end, *our* end, who knew what it would smash into?

The Barnetts of course had no knowledge of any of this as they were shuttled across the tarmac at the Southwestern Spaceport. Their vehicle was an open-aired people-mover, slowly rolling toward the rocket-ship waiting to carry them to the Moon. Byron's eyes widened, his jaw dropped, and his tongue poked out a little as he looked up at the ship's shiny red metalwork, its chromium fins, its gargantuan thrusters.

The Biarritz was no less magnificent on the inside. Inspecting every detail as he boarded, Byron found the ship quite luxurious. The passenger cabin was akin to that of a fancy jetliner, two seats per side. Boarding just behind Byron was his brother, who was less concerned with the attractiveness of the cabin than the faces of the passengers, and one passenger in particular. She looked to be Taji's own age of sixteen, her black hair was long, straight, and glossy, her eyes were the color of the bright green sea around a tropical island, and her skin was slightly sunburnt.

Taji's instant impression was that she was the prettiest girl he'd ever seen—and he'd seen his fair share of pretty girls. In her window seat, she was looking out at the pre-flight activity on the tarmac below.

Next to her, in the aisle seat, sat a tall, bony customer in his twenties wearing a velvet suit in hunter green, a yellow ascot— which is a silk neck scarf looped under the chin—and sparkly diamond cufflinks in his French cuffs. Even more notable than his getup was his accent: an English accent with a weird squeak to it, the kind of accent a cricket might speak with if transformed into a person by an English magician. Taji got an earful of it as the fellow requested from the space-hostess a glass of pomegranate juice with a twig of cinnamon. He was visibly irritated when it was explained to him, apologetically, that *The Biarritz* stocked in its galley neither pomegranate juice nor cinnamon twigs, after which he settled on a diet ginger ale. As the space-hostess stepped away to fill the order, Taji whispered down to this velvet-clad passenger:

"Sorry, but is there any way I could ask you to trade seats with me? I'm right behind you."

The English fellow leaned out of his seat, examined the empty seat behind him, looked up at Taji with a sour expression, and asked:

"Why?"

Taji glanced at the girl of the glossy black hair to the fellow's left—she was still looking out the window, and with her earphones on wasn't hearing any of this. Then Taji gave the English fellow a wink, confessing:

"Because I'd rather ride next to her than my brother."

Supremely bothered, the English fellow sighed like an opera singer, stood up, and took the seat behind him, clearing the way for Taji to sit down.

The girl of the glossy black hair turned away from the window, took off her earphones, and gave her new seatmate a polite smile. Taji wasted no time introducing himself:

"Hiya, my name's Taji."

"I'm Xing-Xing." Her voice was firm but warm, an unusual combination.

"First trip to the Moon?" Taji said.

"First trip to Earth. First trip on my own, I mean."

"You're a Lunarite!"

"I'm a 'Lunarian.' A Lunarite is someone who *lives* on the Moon. A Lunarian is someone who was born there."

"You were born on the Moon? Wa-*wow*! So in the interest of interplanetary friendship, since this is my first trip to your home world, maybe once we get there, you could show me around."

"The Moon's not a world, it's a satellite," Xing-Xing explained pleasantly.

"Well, I'm sure there are *lots* of things about life in space you could teach me," Taji said with a smile.

Usually Xing-Xing didn't find brash boys to her liking, but Taji's self-confidence was strangely amusing, as if he were letting you in on a running joke. Also it didn't hurt that he was so handsome.

"Isn't 'Taji' a Japanese name?" she said a little suspiciously.

"Yup. Japanese and Swahili. Same spelling, no connection. My biological dad was from Kenya."

Xing-Xing liked this. It made this boy a bit interesting.

"So what were you doing on Earth?" Taji said.

"Visiting colleges. I might go a year early, if my father lets me."

"Impressive. I *like* girls with high I.Q.'s."

"But do girls with high I.Q.'s like *you?*"

"Some do, some don't. I try my best either way."

Seeing in her eyes that she was enjoying the chitchat, Taji said:

"Would you be free to go out with me tomorrow night? Saturday night's date night even on the Moon, right?"

"You just sat down and you're already asking me out?" Xing-Xing laughed. "I don't even *know* you!"

"Well, we have the whole ride up to fix *that.*"

Never in her life had Xing-Xing had such a crazy first conversation with *anyone*, let alone a boy. So far though, she wasn't looking to find a way out of it.

But if Taji was beginning to charm Xing-Xing with the power of personality, in the row directly behind them Byron was well into doing the opposite to the English fellow who'd taken Taji's original seat.

The problem was that Byron was now trying to cross over the fellow's knees to get from the window seat back into the aisle. This in itself wouldn't have produced such a scene of turmoil, except that the Englishman's tray-table was down, his briefcase of fake white crocodile leather was resting on top of it, his diet ginger ale was on a cocktail napkin on top of his briefcase, and in his lap was a packet of Space Gazelle Wasabi Nibbles that he'd been munching since the space-hostess had delivered his drink.

With a final tug at his own leg, Byron tumbled into the aisle. Once there he stood up, climbed onto the English fellow's aisle-side armrest, and opened the overhead compartment, where he found José Ignacio stretched out lengthwise, all seven feet and several centimeters of him.

"Ex*cuse* me!" the robot snapped. "I'm napping in here!"

"I just need a pillow!" Byron snapped back.

Mr. and Mrs. Barnett were observing their boys from across the aisle, watching Taji flirt with Xing-Xing and Byron "argue" with his toy robot, which he'd squeezed between carry-on items in the overhead compartment.

"Our two sons," sighed Mrs. Barnett, "girl crazy and plain crazy."

Having now acquired the extra pillow he was after, Byron leapt down off the armrest into the aisle again and worked his way back over the English fellow's knees to the window seat. After adjusting his head support the way he wanted it, he turned to introduce himself.

"My name's Byron Barnett. But you can call me 'Boon.' "

"I'm Lucky von Stroganoff," said the Englishman.

"Really? You don't *look* like a 'Lucky.' "

"You have a good eye."

"Well, what's the matter with you?"

"I nauseate easily. I tend to vomit in space."

"But you're on your way to the Moon. Doesn't that make up for it?"

"I don't much care for the Moon."

"Then why're you going?"

"Papa is a gem dealer and jeweler in London: he buys, cuts, and sells diamonds. And if you want the best diamonds, you have to get on a rocket-ship, now that all the good mines on Earth have been picked clean."

Byron found the Englishman's accent quite nutty, and not only because he was from London. There was the weird squeak to start with, plus which his "r's" all sounded like "w's." Also he seemed to be adding extra syllables to certain words; and when he referred to his father, he pronounced it: "Pa-PAH."

"Is 'von Stroganoff' really an English name?" Byron said, always curious about what people called themselves.

"You also have a good ear," Lucky said. "My great-great-grandpapa was half Russian and half Prussian. But he moved the family to London, so we became Brits. But everybody's something else if you go back far enough."

"Good point."

Lucky wriggled in his seat, rearranging himself to try to get more comfortable. "These trips are agony for me," he said, "but Papa sends me every six months—as punishment for a certain stretch of bad behavior. Why are *you* going?"

"The state of Arizona is sending me up. It's a kinda special program they have."

Lucky nodded several times, because he didn't really have a follow-up question. Byron took the opportunity to keep talking:

"Incidentally, I'm half English myself. My dad's mom and dad came over to Arizona from a place in England called 'Bath.' Ever hear of it?"

"I'm there every other July for the International Convention of Gemologists."

"Ooh, I *love* a good convention. I recently attended ZipperCon."

"And what about your mother's family?"

"Well, my *mom* was born in Bogotá, which in case you're not familiar is the capital of Colombia, which in the event

you're unaware is a country in South America, which if by
some chance you don't—

"I know where South America is."

"Oh, okay. Good. My *abuelos* still live there actually. *Abuelos*
is Spanish for 'grandparents,' in case *no hables español*. And my
great-grandmother, my *bisabuela,* was from Peru, from a town
way up at the tippy-top of the Andes Mountains. So if you do
the math, it's pretty much for sure that I have a fraction of the
Mighty Inka in me. In my chromosomes and whatnot."

"The Mighty Inka?"

"The Mighty Inka. You know, the Emperor of the Inkas
in the olden days."

"Ah. Right."

"Even though people never guess about my whole South
American side, cause my hair color sorta throws 'em off,
plus which my face is fifty percent Anglo-Saxon. But my
mom says my eyes tell the tale. They're dark brown, if
you're wondering, not Halloween black."

Byron held open an eyelid with his fingers and leaned in
to give Lucky a good look—but just now the PA system jingled,
so Lucky raised a hand to put Byron on hold. They listened to
the announcement together: Byron eagerly, Lucky with a deep
sense of dread about what was coming.

*"Ladies and Gentlemen, this is Captain Jay Swizzler. We've
been cleared for lift-off, so now's the time to sit back, buckle up,
and enjoy the ride."*

A minute later the ship was rotating upright on its
launching pad and Byron's grin was rotating out of his lips
… until he didn't so much have a smile on his face as a face
on his smile. For him this was like the rise of a roller coaster
before it curled over its apex and plunged into its loops. Soon
he and his fellow passengers had rotated ninety degrees,

heads back, feet up. And then came the moment Byron had waited his entire life for …

The Biarritz was a mighty marvel as it blasted off the surface of the Earth, streaming fire from its giant thrusters. Inside the ship, g-forces were twisting faces, but Byron didn't mind. With his forehead pressed against the window, he watched as the ship rose through:

* the troposphere (shooting past a supersonic jet) …
* the stratosphere (streaking by a weather balloon) …
* the mesosphere (crossing paths with a falling star) …
* the thermosphere (speeding past The Ritz Orbital, a fancy space-hotel)
* and the exosphere (rising right between two crisscrossing satellites).

The atomic technology powering rockets such as this was unfortunately not advanced enough to carry passengers beyond the limits of the solar system: humankind had not yet cracked the conundrum of how people could travel from one star to the next; but *inside* the solar system, that celestial collection of eight planets whizzing in their orbits around the sun, an atomic rocket was still the last word in transportation. Being an actual passenger on this top-of-the-line vehicle had Byron jumping for joy—just without moving.

The Biarritz entered space. With the stars beginning to glitter, the ship leveled off. Byron's face was still glued to the window, and he'd been quietly giggling for almost a minute. Finally he turned to Lucky to share his excitement. But even though Lucky had survived takeoff without too much trouble, he was starting to feel nauseated. He grabbed his space-sickness pouch and puked it full. His vomitus was bright green, due to the Wasabi Nibbles he'd recently

snacked on. Byron felt bad for him, but was happy to confirm by comparison that his own stomach was rock solid. In
fact, his stomach and other major body parts were feeling
better than normal. Space travel agreed with him.

The PA system jingled again, and Captain Swizzler
announced:

*"Ladies and gentlemen, we've reached our cruising speed of
a hundred thousand miles per hour, which makes a little over two
and a half hours of flying time to the Moon. The sailing looks
smooth tonight, so we expect to put in right on schedule. And for
those of you on the left side of the cabin, we have an extra treat
this evening: Comet Khayyam—named for Omar Khayyam, the
great Persian astronomer, mathematician and poet—coming into
view just about now."*

Byron spotted it before the captain's last words were out
of his mouth. The comet's fuzzy head of ice and dust and its
long, frosty tail were a hundred times bigger and a thousand
times sharper than any such celestial body Byron had ever
seen from Earth. Viewed from the comfort of *The Biarritz*,
such a feast of space-sights as these made it easy to believe
that the cosmos was pure splendor. After all, all Byron or
anyone else aboard this rocket-ship could see out their window was beauty, not danger.

But time was running short now. A white worm's rear end
was about to pop out of nowhere and into the spatial neighbor-
hood, and a barrage of meteoroids was about to come shooting
through it. Yet not a soul in the solar system knew ...

For Byron, mesmerized by the outer-space spectacle, it seemed the blink of an eye before *The Biarritz* had reached its destination and the Moon was looming large through his window, though the elapsed time since blast-off was two hours and thirty-four minutes.

"*And ladies and gentleman,*" Captain Swizzler announced through the PA, "*in just a few moments we'll be landing in beautiful downtown Cosmopolis, where the local time is three minutes past midnight and the temperature is a brisk, negative two hundred and four degrees Fahrenheit. Hope you remembered your mittens!*"

Byron was getting his first good look at the Moon's palette of silvers, platinums, shiny grays, and inky blacks. *The Biarritz's* landing lights were reflected in the regolith below, which as Byron had learned on his way to the Southwestern Spaceport is the correct name for the powdery top layer of lunar "soil."

Next the ship passed over: a mile-high mountain range ... a gorge and surrounding ringwall of Grand Canyonesque proportions ... boulders the size of dumptrucks and some as big as buildings.

The lunar colony came into view up ahead: Cosmopolis, a cluster of brightly lit domes, including a central dome as large as Arizona City's whole City Center, over which rose a control tower topped with a big bubble of super-strong glass. People in Cosmopolis called it the "orb."

The Biarritz pivoted into an upright position over the West Landing Zone, then descended, landing with what Byron felt was a very tolerable bump. A metal framework rose up hydraulically, locked onto the rocket from bottom to top, and slowly tipped it down to a horizontal position. Then an enclosed gangplank of transparent plastic moved forward, connecting to the ship.

Passengers disembarked. The Barnett family was in the middle of the line, except for Byron, who kept slowing down to study the lunar surface through the clear gangplank and in so doing ended up at the very back. Not only the regolith had captured his interest, but also the specialized cannons located at twenty-yard intervals around every dome of the city, mounted on pivoting platforms and notable for their corkscrew-shaped barrels.

At the far end of the gangplank Byron caught up with his family in the reception area, where right away they noticed an important-looking gentleman of Asian ancestry, with what seemed to be three assistants standing behind him, holding walkie-talkies and clipboards.

"I think that's Governor Tang," Mr. Barnett whispered to Mrs. Barnett.

"Daddy!" Xing-Xing called out.

She ran ahead and gave her father a long hug hello. Then she made introductions:

"Daddy, this is Taji Barnett and his family. Mr. and Mrs. Barnett, this is my father, Jing Tang, Governor of the Moon. Daddy, Mr. Barnett is the new engineer from Amalgamated MegaPhysics."

Taji had learned on the flight up that Xing-Xing's father was Chinese by birth and her late mother had been an Italian lady who grew up in a palace on a Venice canal and took a boat to school every day even though she lived in a city! But Xing-Xing hadn't mentioned her father's job. Looking at him now, seeing his diplomatic haircut and outstanding posture, it was easy to tell he was a dignitary. In fact he came from a long line of dignitaries: Chinese statesmen and ambassadors, of which he himself was the first extra-planetary example.

"Mr. Governor," said Mr. Barnett, "how do you do?"

The governor shook Mr. Barnett's hand. "When I made the call to AmPhys," he said, "I told them, 'Don't bother putting anyone less than your top man on a rocket-ship! Because the Lunar League only hires the very best.' "

"Well, Mr. Governor, the *top* top man left the firm a few years back, so I'd have to say I moved up by default."

"Don't be modest, Barnett—I've seen your résumé. And Mrs. Barnett ... what a vision of loveliness! Welcome to Cosmopolis."

Before Mrs. Barnett could answer, she felt Byron tugging at her skirt.

"Mom, can we go for a tour?"

"Sweetheart, it's after midnight. I don't think we can expect the good people of the Moon to accommodate us this late."

"I tell you what, Byron," said Governor Tang, "you go get a good night's sleep, and first thing in the morning, I'll give you the tour myself."

Byron's alarm clock chirped at the crack of 7 a.m., but even though his eyes were closed, his brain was already up. Keeping his eyes shut tight, he grimaced as if in pain, or as if expecting to be in pain any second. Then he begged out loud:

"Please let it not be a dream."

Little by little he opened one eye until, through a port-hole-window a foot thick, he saw the blue dot of Earth out in space, at the edge of the lunar horizon. In a burst of joy he jumped up, ran to the window, confirmed it was Earth through a telescope, swiveled the telescope until he found a lunar crater, then focused in on two mooncrawlers—which were bulldozer-type mining machines. Turning away from the telescope, he danced a jig around the room, singing:

"I'm living on the Moon! The Moon is my legal address! I'm lunar! I'm lunacious! I'm a lunatic!"

Suddenly he realized how hungry he was: no doubt a side effect of travel by rocket-ship that no one had warned him about. He dropped to his knees, yanked his suitcase out from under his bed, and rummaged in it for an unopened variety pack of Space Gazelle Space Cakes. It was supposed to be his emergency supply, but such is life.

Finding it, he used a fingernail to slice into the plastic wrap and, once he'd gotten the box out and ripped off its top, considered which of his top three flavors—Chocolate Comet, Coconut Creation, or Big Bang Banana—would best prime his stomach for its first full day in space. But in a burst of originality he settled on his *fourth* favorite flavor: Venusian Vanilla. He used his teeth to tear open the foil, then broke the Cake in two, gobbled half, folded the foil tightly over the other half and stashed it in his belt buckle's secret compartment for subsequent consumption.

And that's when he caught sight of José Ignacio still asleep in the bedroom's second twin bed. He marched over and jerked the blanket right off him.

"Get up, you negligent gadget! We've got a busy day!"

Seen from above, Cosmopolis was a snowflake of domes connected by sparkling white tubeways. On this, the morning after the Barnetts' arrival on the Moon, though still less than ten hours since *The Biarritz* had touched down, the family was walking through one such tubeway: Governor Tang was giving them the tour.

Byron was in another one of his trances. The sights and sounds of the lunar colony—not to mention the fact that the air here smelled like hot buttered popcorn—had laid claim to his imagination so completely that he was absentmindedly dragging his toy robot behind him on its cord: not once did he turn to have a word with the full-sized José Ignacio, not once did José Ignacio pop up beside him to pepper him with questions or comments.

Also here for the tour was Xing-Xing: she was walking with Taji behind the rest of group, the two of them more interested in each other than the excursion itself. With the governor leading the way, the Barnetts hit all the colony's hot spots, starting with the Hydroponics Dome. Here fruits and vegetables grew in long trays of nutrient solution: carrots, blueberries, snow peas, sweet potatoes, kale, kumquats, bananas, squash. Not to mention all the legumes: lentils, chickpeas, alfalfa, broad beans, pinto beans, navy beans, and—thank goodness—allergen-free peanuts.

Next to Hydroponics was the Worship Dome, a one-hundred-percent white space with a hologram-generator in the middle. The governor rotated a dial on its control board, holographically switching the dome's innards from a Baptist meetinghouse to a Jewish synagogue to a Muslim mosque to a Hindu temple to a Tibetan temple to a Native American sacred place to a Shinto shrine—and finally to a Catholic cathedral.

All faiths were welcome here, the governor said, and they would be glad to add additional holograms upon request. As a matter of fact, the very first family of Zoroastrians to move to the Moon had arrived on board *The Biarritz* along with the Barnetts, and a flameproof chamber within the Worship Dome was in the works to accommodate the Zoroastrian use of fire as a focal point for prayer.

Next stop: the Arts Dome. Here many activities of the aesthetic variety were going on, including but not limited to:

* a painter dabbing at his canvas (he said he was painting the Oyster Nebula five thousand light years from Earth—though to Byron's eye it was just a big blue blob, or at best a blue jellyfish);

* a sculptor chiseling a large moon rock, with a young lady in a golden spacesuit posing beside it (good luck dipping that rock in molten gold, Byron thought);

* a kindergarten class building a life-sized skeleton of a *Tyrannosaurus rex* out of Styrofoam (this was the kind of artwork that Byron could get behind);

* a ceramics instructor demonstrating how to make a vase (which Byron found controversial, since there were precious few flowers on the Moon).

Then came the Miners' Dome. This was more accurately a diamond exchange where buyers and sellers haggled over prices for gems. Lunar diamonds sparkled in their glass cases, each case containing a different color of stone, including the Moon's signature blue-white diamonds, but also pink diamonds, yellow diamonds, violet diamonds, and even emerald-lookalike green diamonds.

Byron spotted Lucky von Stroganoff examining a gem through his loupe, which is the little magnifying glass that watchmakers and jewelers use. Lucky looked up a moment later and gave Byron a wave but was apparently too busy to step away for a chat.

Meanwhile, Mr. Barnett turned around to find his wife holding a pair of pink diamonds the size of cherries up to her earlobes. She made a face as if to say, "How fabulous do these look on me?!"; but Mr. Barnett turned out his pockets and shrugged, as if to answer, "Forgive me, love of my life, but I'm all out of cash!" Mrs. Barnett blew Mr. Barnett a kiss anyway, then she handed the diamonds back to the gem merchant behind his case and moved along.

After this the group took an autowalk through a tubeway toward Central Dome. En route, Mr. and Mrs. Barnett told Governor Tang how impressed they were with Cosmopolis, both architecturally and in its interior design. The city was so bright, clean, and uncluttered, and made from such a stylish array of plastics and formicas. Just as the autowalk deposited them at the door to Central Dome, the very hub of the lunar city, the governor replied:

"And I've saved the best for last."

They stepped inside. Central Dome was vast, the size of three, maybe four, possibly even five soccer stadiums. With its real grass, hillocks, and palm trees, it might have been a park in a megalopolis on Earth, except for the starscape overhead, visible through the dome's super-tempered glass.

In the center of it all was a food court with a French bistro, a Lebanese eatery, an Argentinian grill, a Russian cafeteria, an Italian trattoria, a sushi bar, a french fry stand, and a soda shop, all with "outdoor" as well as "indoor" tables.

Byron was particularly glad to see a Space Gazelle sign hanging in the soda shop window. The Gazelle was pictured floating through the cosmic deep in its clear-plastic spacesuit, but instead of celestial objects all around, there were ice cream cones.

The message was clear: Space Gazelle Ice Cream was served here! Byron silently expressed his appreciation for this godsend of refreshments—and for the good sense of whoever did the ordering at Cosmopolis Food Services. Then he said a little prayer for his favorite flavors to all be in stock, which in order of importance were:

* Dark Matter Mango
* Star Cluster Strawberry
* Planetary Pistachio
* Light-Speed Lemon
* Black Hole Black Walnut
* Chocolate Mint Magnetic Field
* Nebula Nectarine
* and Blue Moon Butter Pecan.

(The secret ingredient that made Space Gazelle's ice cream so superb was rumored to be ice from real comets, though Galactic Snacking Solutions understandably kept the recipe under lock and key.)

With Byron calculating what time it was back in Arizona—trying to work out whether he could make the argument to his mother that his stomach still thought it was in a time zone where it wasn't too early in the day for an ice cream soda—a pair of cyclists sped by on the bikepath. Further along they zipped past a bunch of kids reading comics on a grassy hill before circling a little amphitheater where a singer with a guitar was entertaining a small audience with that novelty song that just wouldn't go away, *Outer Space Sweetie Face*.

"This is where we have fun," said Governor Tang.

Byron eyed a cluster of statuary, including four heroic figures in bronze: one of a dog, three of human beings. The governor elucidated:

"The dog is Laika, the first living being to orbit the Earth, aboard Sputnik 2. And this is Neil Armstrong, first man to walk on the Moon. And here we have J. Marcus Mingus, aka 'Moonbeard Marc,' the first man to make a million credits off-

Earth, though of course no one can say what happened to him *or* his fortune in the end, since, as you know, he disappeared. And last but not least, Sfiso Mahlobo, President of South Africa until he resigned to become the first head of the Lunar League and first Governor of the Moon, the man who set the standard for civilized existence in space. We owe him a lot."

Byron was still stuck on the statue of Moonbeard Marc. In bronze he looked just as eccentric as he had in black and white in *The Story of the Moon*, but you wouldn't have expected less from an old-timer who braided his hair and beard with lunar diamonds. Hence the "Moonbeard" in "Moonbeard Marc." Over the statue's head was a sculpted burst of fireworks, a reminder of the commonly held belief that it was Moonbeard Marc who, every year on his birthday, had shot fireworks into the lunar sky from some secret location, for seven years after he vanished.

Not far from the statuary Byron spotted more of those specialized cannons with their corkscrew barrels that he'd been noticing everywhere around the colony, only this time mounted on pivoting platforms *inside* the dome.

"What're all the cannons for?" he asked the governor.

"We call them 'goo-guns.' They fire high-viscosity resin. In case a meteoroid ever strikes a dome, we'd shoot at the hole to seal it up. But don't worry, Byron, our radar-net reaches all the way to Neptune: we'd have plenty of warning of any incoming meteoroid and more than enough time to blast it to bits out in space: these guns are only an extreme precaution."

Just now two teenage boys flew overhead, wearing plastic wings measuring six feet from tip to tip.

"Rabiznaz!" Byron blurted as an after-whoosh of wind brushed his face. ("Rabiznaz," of course, was "Zanzibar" backwards, a word Byron used when needing to express double the usual amazement.)

"And that's our favorite sport," said Governor Tang. "We turn off the artificial gravity here in Central Dome on Saturday mornings, which is why you're feeling the spring in your step at the moment. You're experiencing one sixth Earth gravity, so once you've been fitted with lightweight wings, your muscles are strong enough to create lift and propulsion. It's not just gliding, it's actual flying."

Byron could not take his eyes off the two humans in the air: soaring, swooping, swirling. With a jolt, it occurred to him to ask:

"Can I try?"

"I'm not sure you quite meet the height requirement," the governor said. "Let's have a look." He guided Byron to the height chart, measured him, shook his head. "Almost. I'd say you'll be ready in a few months. But Taji, if *you'd* like to try, I'm sure Xing-Xing wouldn't mind showing you how it's done. In the meantime, I think I have something else Byron might be interested in."

Xing-Xing said to Taji:

"Let's see how well your muscles work on the Moon."

Taji liked the sound of this. He winked at Byron (who had no idea what his brother was winking about), then went off with Xing-Xing. The governor turned back to Byron.

"So. Ready for your first day of school?"

Byron's whole body tensed up. "You have to go to school here on the *weekend?*"

"Usually no, but you've arrived on a very special day. The Moon's rotation means we have two weeks of nighttime followed by two weeks of daylight. And on the switchover, there's always a class fieldtrip: out on the surface."

Byron's horror flipped to bliss. Not twenty minutes later he found himself in an airlock in the Cosmopolis Department of Transporation, together with a dozen other kids, all of them suiting up in actual silver spacesuits and clear bubble-helmets. Also here was the young Inuit lady who would be Byron's teacher, Miss Ahlooloo, originally from Alaska but a Lunarite of four years now. She stepped over to Byron to show him the hidden zippers on his suit, but Byron had already found every one of them on his own.

The kids began boarding their bus: a square, all-glass vehicle built to move on a continuous metal track like a tank. Mounted on top was a four-wheeled rover that could be brought down on a retractrable ramp and used for zipping around craters and such. Engineers referred to it as an "LRV," short for "Lunar Roving Vehicle," but most Lunarites just called it a "moon buggy."

Meanwhile, the rest of the Barnetts were in the Department of Transportation's visitors' area, looking into the airlock through a viewport, watching as Byron, seated inside the bus, waved at them with a big grin on his face.

"Are you sure this is safe?" Mrs. Barnett asked Governor Tang.

"The children are in very good hands with Miss Ahlooloo. And it's best Byron jump right in, it'll help him get rid of his fears."

"Get *rid* of his fears? I've been working his whole life to get some fears *into* him!"

The tall doors of the airlock opened, and the lunar school bus began to move, rolling slowly onto the surface of the Moon. From his window seat, with José Ignacio beside him, Byron could plainly see that great events were about to occur in his life. What was less obvious was how perilous many of these same events would be. Because thirty seconds earlier, somewhere in the solar system a white worm's rear end had appeared, and through it was now shooting a flood of meteoroids like boulder-sized bullets through an intergalactic gun.

CHAPTER: 6

THE LUNAR SCHOOL BUS rolled tank-like out of its airlock in the Cosmopolis Department of Transportation and onto the surface of the Moon. Next to Byron sat his robotic crony, José Ignacio, the pair of them peering out the glass-paneled bus at the silvery regolith, a word that Byron, as a newly minted Lunarite, was quickly growing very fond of, a word meaning the top layer of powder covering the Moon's stratum of solid rock. "Regolith."

Several carrot-colored mooncrawlers were bulldozing nearby, alongside one mammoth rockcrusher, a vehicle the shape of a grasshopper but the size of an elephant, with an enclosed cockpit up top for its operator to sit in. Byron watched as a rockcrusher's front arms came down hard and smashed a boulder to bits, which a mooncrawler promptly scooped up for transport. Then the rockcrusher's operator spotted the school bus and ceased his crushing long enough to wave hello.

Byron raised his own hand and asked:

"Miss Ahlooloo, are they mining diamonds?"

Intead of answering, Miss Ahlooloo turned to a girl of Byron's age by the name of Honeybun Bajpai. The first thing you would've noticed about Honeybun if you'd been watching her get ready back in the airlock at Cosmopolis a few minutes earlier was that she'd taken off the pink-and-gold, over-the-shoulder sash from her sari (which is a kind of attractively draped garment that female persons in India tend to wear) and put it back on *over* her spacesuit, adding a delightful stripe of color to the otherwise black-and-white lunar fashion routine. Also her ski-goggle glasses, which typically make a person look slightly zany, somehow made Honeybun look quite cute, even inside her spacesuit helmet.

But it wasn't her looks that made her really stand out, it was what you *couldn't* tell about her just using your eyeballs: she was a genius! No surprise really, since her whole family was abnormally smart. Her parents—who she'd moved up to the Moon with from Jaipur the year before—were both doctors, her mother a brain surgeon and her father a space-allergist. Anyway, Honeybun was not only the best student in Miss Ahlooloo's class, she was the best student in the history of the lunar school system. She could always be relied on to keep the conversation going with an accurate fact or figure, which is why teachers liked calling on her whenever there was an informational gap happening. As in right now:

"Honeybun, would you care to answer Byron's question?"

"The diamond miners still work by hand," Honeybun told Byron in an accent that sounded a little like singing— and in a very friendly voice. She was the kind of individual, you realized pretty fast, who most likely knew more than you did about whatever the topic was that was being discussed, but she never made you feel uninformed; instead she always made you feel like you were finding out something new at exactly the right moment to know it.

"These vehicles and their operators are mining oxygen," Honeybun said. "They use a hydrogen reduction process to extract fresh air from moon rocks. You're breathing the result right now."

Byron sucked in a deep, noisy breath, then exhaled with a whistle. "Refreshing!" he said.

By pure coincidence, half a mile away in Central Dome, Taji Barnett was at this very moment saying the very same thing, after Xing-Xing had just explained to *him* the basics of oxygen production at Cosmopolis, oxygen being the lunar colony's number-one concern at all times. As they discussed the ins and outs of it, Xing-Xing finished strapping Taji into his set of plastic wings, since they were gearing up for flight.

"Ready, Earth-boy?"

"Ready like confetti."

"Confetti? How is confetti ready?"

"You know, like you're at a surprise party waiting for the birthday girl to show up, holding your fistful of confetti, all set to throw it at her when she walks in the door, to commence the fiesta. Ready like confetti."

Without commenting on the dubious simile, Xing-Xing turned away from Taji, sprinted a few yards, jumped, and flew up into the dome's airspace, using her wings in graceful bursts. Taji followed her lead. Since Xing-Xing had been doing this for years, she was elegant in the air; but Taji was a natural athlete, and he took to the new sport on the spot. Together they swooped and swirled, starry space above them on the other side of the dome, green grass and hillocks below on the dome's floor.

"Hey, Moon-girl! How's this?" Taji executed an impressive loop-de-loop. "Don't be afraid to say 'magnificent!'"

Xing-Xing smiled at his swagger, then flew straight up toward the roof of the dome. She was heading for a small aerie there, which was only visible from halfway up. Taji, naturally, flapped his wings and followed.

In the Barnett family's quarters, Mrs. Barnett was by this time sizing up her weekend's work. She was in the kitchen unpacking her china, which she'd insisted on bringing along as a condition for agreeing to move to the Moon, because she had no intention of eating off somebody else's plates in her own home.

As she checked each piece for chips or cracks, she mentally divided up her next several tasks in order of importance and degree of difficulty. Also she was thinking about how to redecorate. At two thousand square feet, their quarters were spacious enough, and the rooms flowed nicely; but the place needed an across-the-board overhaul in interior design, and she was just the woman for the job.

She was still musing over colors and fabrics when she went into Byron's bedroom to unpack his clothes and hang them in the closet. Here her mind shifted over to Byron himself, and she put her eye to his telescope at the porthole-window. She didn't really expect to catch a glimpse of Byron's class on the regolith, but there was the lunar school bus, maybe a mile away, a glassy box glinting in starlight as it rolled slowly along. Spotting it made Mrs. Barnett feel better than had been the case for the last several hours; because even though she hadn't mentioned it to anyone, she'd had a nagging feeling of doom all morning long.

Only a minute later, the school bus reached its destination and came to a stop. Miss Ahlooloo gave her students final instructions and reviewed all the safety precautions one last time. Then they were ready.

Byron let his classmates exit the bus first, not because he was nervous about going outside, but because he didn't want anyone behind him rushing him along. Byron was a person who preferred doing things at his own pace. Most of the time very fast, but once in a while quite slow. Right now, for instance, speed was not his prime concern. He wanted to savor the experience as he descended the small ladder on the side of the bus that would bring him to the surface of the Moon …

With each step down, his anticipation of placing his foot in the soft moondust rose. At the last rung of the ladder he leapt off and hit the regolith with both feet at the same time. The moment of contact was spine-tingling, unlike any step Byron had ever taken before or expected ever to take again.

He walked a few feet, then turned back to examine his footprints in the regolith: they were lighter in color than the rest of the radiation-darkened "topsoil."

He spun around to take in the view of a mile-high mountain peak and a mile-low impact crater. With no atmosphere to soften the views, everything was razor-sharp in the distance. The lunar horizon was so close and clear that it precisely divided the Moon's surface from starry space—and from the shining orb of Earth beyond.

Next Byron tested out the laws of physics as applied to his own body by letting himself fall face-forward from a standing position: before hitting the ground he had plenty of time to put out his hands, break his fall, and push himself back up. This was due to the fact that, as Governor Tang had pointed out, the Moon's gravity was only one sixth the gravity back home: a delightful detail of lunar living that would make time spent here quite interesting.

Spotting a boulder that would've weighed way too much for him to lift in Arizona, Byron laid his gloved hands on it and hoisted it over his head, grinning at his own lunar superstrength.

"*I can do that on Earth,*" quipped José Ignacio.

The robot was standing right behind Byron, transmitting

directly into Byron's helmet intercom. Byron swung around and flung the boulder straight at him, knocking him down. But José Ignacio easily righted himself by digging both claws into the regolith and extending his arms, leaving a perfect imprint of his robotic body in the moondust.

Miss Ahlooloo now checked her watch and addressed the class through their intercoms:

"Ready, everyone? Daylight is about to strike!"

Byron watched the sharp line of daylight hit the mountains in the distance as it moved in their direction. Since there was no air to diffuse sunlight, it was an instantaneous difference between night and day along the Day-Night Terminator Line. Nothing like on Earth, where day breaks slowly in the sky and night sinks away like light down a funnel. Here the switchover happened all at once!

The moving flank of sunlight triggered a phosphorescent effect in the regolith, causing minerals to light up and sparkle until it looked like the Moon was covered by ten trillion tons of crushed diamonds. The advancing line of daylight reached Byron, bathing him in brilliance and lighting up the ground all around him.

"Byron," said Miss Ahlooloo via intercom, *you can keep up with it, if you like. Just don't go over the ridge.*"

Byron shot off, chasing the advancing line of daylight, moving ahead of it with big, lunar strides. Hearing him giggle via the open intercom link, Miss Ahlooloo smiled at her new pupil's get-up-and-go. Also she was amused by the toy robot bouncing along behind him, hooked to his spacesuit by cord. From Byron's perspective, of course, it was a seven-foot-and-several-centimeters José Ignacio bounding alongside him—until José Ignacio lengthened his leaps by dialing up his boot jets and flying ahead.

"*Hey!*" Byron hollered. "*Wait up, you pretentious appliance!*"

José Ignacio did not wait up. Byron only caught up to him when the robot stopped at the top of a ridge. From here, looking down, they could take in the whole canyon below.

"*Zanzibar!*" Byron whispered.

"*What?*" José Ignacio said, hearing in Byron's voice that he wasn't commenting only on the view. "*What are you looking at?*"

"*What are the odds?*" Byron said.

"*What are the odds of WHAT? What's down there?*"

"*Don't you see it?*"

José Ignacio scanned the canyon floor, but sometimes a boy's brain is just plain better than a robot's cranium at spotting the item of utmost importance.

"*It's Rattlesnake Rill!*" Byron said. "*Right there!*"

José Ignacio zeroed in on the tiny bit of moonscape below that Byron was pointing at (and which, by the way, in Byron's mind—by way of Byron's memory, by way of his colorized moon poster in his room back in Arizona—was lit up the color of cotton-candy pink)—and there, indeed, was the snake-like groove that Byron was referring to: Rattlesnake Rill, in actual fact.

"*If I know what you're thinking,*" José Ignacio warned, "*and I always DO know—stop it!*"

"*You have no idea what I'm thinking!*"

"*You're thinking you want to go DOWN there!*"

"*Exactly!*"

"*We can't!*"

"*We HAVE to!*"

"*We're not authorized! We're not equipped! We're not even organized!*"

José Ignacio's argument would have been stronger if he could've added that back at Cosmopolis, in the command center atop the control tower, trouble was brewing which in a matter of minutes would require the field trip to be cut short and Miss Ahlooloo's class to climb back into the bus and hurry home.

But José Ignacio was not in touch with the command center, where an alarm had just started ringing. On the big screen was a picture of the solar system taken telescopically a moment earlier: the alarm corresponded to a blinking yellow dot just past Saturn.

The governor's deputy and right-hand-man, twenty-eight-year-old Canutus Olafsson, sprang into action, double-checking every circuit in the system to be sure the alarm was no glitch. Six feet eleven inches tall, with white-blond hair down to his shoulders, blond eyebrows, and a ready-to-chase-the-ball look always in his eyes, Deputy Olafsson seemed like a golden retriever running around on hind legs. A golden retriever, that is, who beyond his canine-sharp reflexes and doggy-powered energy levels also knew what a blinking yellow dot on a telescreen actually *meant*.

After finishing his technical checks and confirming that the alarm system was in good working order, he took the elevator down to the bottom of the control tower and headed quickly into Cosmopolis proper. Here he intercepted Governor Tang leaving Central Dome with Mr. Barnett. In a low voice he informed the governor:

"Sir, we may be in for some trouble."

Six minutes later, Governor Tang, Mr. Barnett, and Deputy Olafsson were in the control tower elevator rising toward the orb, the governor asking questions all the way up:

"Why was there no warning? Is the radar-net offline?"

"The distortion came out of nowhere," Deputy Olafsson said. "And the meteoroids shooting through it show no sign of stopping anytime soon." In a worried voice, he added: "Sir, we think it's a white worm."

"I'm a diplomat by training, Canutus, not an astrophysicist —what the devil is a white worm?"

"In theory it's a phenomenon created by the collapse of a supernova with a glut of overcharged quarks at its core. It has properties of a black hole on one end and a worm hole in the middle—which means it can tunnel through space-time itself. By firing rays of gravitation out of its front orifice, it's able to capture objects the size of small planets, pull them all the way through its body, and shoot them out its super-charged *rear* orifice." (Deputy Olafsson was using the word "orifice" instead of "anus" because he thought "anus" sounded too rude to be saying to his boss's face. Both words are correct, so let's not make a thing of it.)

"But are we talking about a living creature?" the governor said. "Is it alive?"

"No, sir, it's a force of nature. Which means it's even more menacing, because it has no mind to control it. Making the danger random and unpredictable."

The elevator doors opened, depositing the three men in the command center, the very cockpit of lunar operations. The "orb."

"Can we patch into a live feed off a probe?" the governor asked after glancing at the picture on the big screen, which wasn't enough information to tell them what they needed to know.

"Already working on it, sir!" a technician fiddling at switches called out. "There!"

The picture of the solar system was replaced by a live shot in black-and-white, relayed by a series of unmanned probes moving outward from Earth. Now they all saw it: a massive, wormy-shaped, silvery-white celestial object near Saturn was expelling large quantities of meteoroids, a veritable tsunami of space-rocks, or a rocky space-tsunami if you prefer.

Suddenly there was a bit of luck: the Red Planet's gravity grabbed the meteoroids as if in an invisible net and swung them away from the general direction of Earth.

"Mars gravity caught it!" shouted Deputy Olafsson.

All eleven people in the command center exhaled in relief. Until Mars's lopsided outer moon, Deimos, locked onto the white worm's rocky spew with its own gravitational force and swung it back in Earth's general direction again. Eleven people gasped: this was now a major emergency.

"Overlay a course projection," ordered Governor Tang.

The technician worked at his panel, causing a line of dots to come up on-screen, predicting the meteoroids' trajectory: not only the Moon, but Cosmopolis itself!

"My God," whispered the governor, "it's heading straight *for* us."

"Sir, there's not enough time to get our rockets aloft," Deputy Olafsson explained, "and too many meteoroids to shoot down even if we tried."

"Sound the alarm," instructed the governor. "Get everyone underground."

"What about my *son?*" said Mr. Barnett. "And the other children on the fieldtrip?!"

"They're outside the trajectory zone. They're safer than *we* are."

Indeed, at this very moment, Byron was not only safe but quite factually jumping for joy, moving in great, low-gravity leaps down a lunar ridge and toward Rattlesnake Rill. José Ignacio, flying beside him, was berating him by intercom:

"This is madness!"

"This is science!"

"Why am I sure that no adult in the solar system would agree with that?!"

"Why am I sure I don't care?!"

They hit the canyon floor. Rattlesnake Rill was only fifty yards away: they made a dash for it. But the rill was less sensational up-close than from a distance: it was, in fact, only a four-foot-deep trench in the ground. The rattlesnakeiness of it disappeared altogether when you were standing in it, as Byron was doing now. He had no intention of admitting his disappointment to José Ignacio, however. Then something caught his eye which all of a sudden made this mini-expedition worth the trouble. From where he was standing, he had a view straight to the bottom of the canyon wall, and there, dead ahead, he saw a shadowy nook in the rock that gave every indication of being the entrance to a cave.

"José Ignacio, do you see what I'm seeing?"

This time the robot had no trouble spotting what Byron was looking at. *"No more cliffs, no more caverns, no more caves!"* he said. *"You promised your mother! I was there! I heard you say it!"*

"No caves on EARTH! I didn't say anything about caves on the MOON! Lunar spelunking was not discussed, ergo was not prohibited! Do you know nothing about the law?!"

Byron leapt out of the rill and made a run for the canyon wall. José Ignacio went after him, trying to stop him with every argument that his logic board could generate. But Byron's mind was already made up. They arrived in under a minute at the nook in question, which as Byron had suspected and as luck would have it was, in point of fact, the entrance to a cave.

"I'm going in," Byron said.

"*Stop or I'll shoot!*" warned José Ignacio.

Ignoring him, Byron snapped the built-in flashlight off his spacesuit, turned it on, and took a step into the cave.

José Ignacio zapped him from behind with a voltage-ray. Byron turned around and stepped back out of the cave's mouth to say:

"*You're losing juice, old chap: I barely felt that.*"

"*And you're losing brain function, old kook! This is demented! It's too dangerous!*'

"*I welcome danger! I send danger a telegram that says where to meet me! When we see each other, I run up and give danger a hug!*"

"*I thought you spat in danger's face.*"

"*Listen: you can either wait for me here where it's 'safe' or come in with me where it's fun! But either way, I'm not leaving this perfectly good cave unexplored!*"

José Ignacio sighed vividly before giving in and following Byron inside. Had they looked up before going forward, they would've seen the incoming flood of meteoroids, now mere moments from reaching Cosmopolis. But they didn't look up, so they had no idea.

They weren't the only ones out of the loop. Back in Central Dome, colonists were fleeing to the sound of alarms going off; but up above the panic, way up in the very apex of the dome, in the secluded aerie, Xing-Xing and Taji were enjoying each other's company, oblivious to the commotion below. They were seated in the aerie's titanium rafters, right up against the super-tempered glass separating them from starry space. This meant they were also at least two hundred yards from the ground below—well out of range of the alarm bells.

"You can't resist me, can you?" Taji said, playing out the flirty fun that had been going on between them all morning. "That's why you brought me up here. To get me alone."

"I brought you here to show you a scenic spot," Xing-Xing said. "You're a new citizen of the Lunar League, I'm just offering a little Lunarian hospitality."

"On a related point: you never answered my question about going out with me tonight. It's Saturday morning. Date night's only eight hours away. You're taking a huge risk by not locking me in."

"My life won't come to an end if I don't go out tonight."

"But your life might really start if you *do*."

Xing-Xing's jaw dropped at Taji's interpersonal daring. But before she could comment, Taji dared even more:

"I have an idea. I'll give you a kiss right now, and depending on whether you like it, you can rule me in or out for tonight."

"Hmmmmm," Xing-Xing said, with a very long "mmmmm" at the end—as if she were weighing the pros and cons of it.

"But I mean, if you don't *want* a test kiss from me," Taji said, "that's fine too. I know the dos and don'ts of dating. And I certainly don't want a 'do' if you're thinking 'don't.' "

Xing-Xing had to admit to herself that she found this boy ridiculously irresistible. Or possibly irresistibly ridiculous. Either way, she couldn't deny that she liked him. "Well," she said, "since I'm already being hospitable … I guess … sure, why not."

She leaned in to give him a better angle to kiss her by; but to get close enough he still had to wrap his plastic wings around her, which they both found quite pleasant. Then, very gently, he pressed his lips to hers. It was going along well for several seconds, until Xing-Xing suddenly pulled back.

"I felt a tremor."

"That's what *all* the girls say."

Taji smiled; Xing-Xing did not. And that's when a meteoroid the size of a watermelon smashed through the roof of Central

Dome not twenty yards from the aerie. Taji's wings were sucked right off his back and went flying straight out the hole. The vacuum-effect yanked at Taji too, pulling him out of the rafters. But he grabbed hold of a metal beam ten yards from the hole into open space and clung tight.

"Just hang on!" shouted Xing-Xing over the din of rushing air. She leapt off the aerie and dove straight down.

"Xing-Xing! Where are you *going*?! This is not a good time to break up with me!"

Pulling out of her dive at the last possible second, Xing-Xing landed beside a goo-gun on the floor of the dome and leapt into the gunner's seat. She flicked open the canon's control box and, using its tiny joystick, swiveled the massive corkscrew-shaped barrel upright. She aimed through the crosshairs and fired.

A stream of gooey sealant in bright metallic purple shot from the cannon and didn't stop shooting until Xing-Xing released the trigger. Her aim was perfect: the goo whizzed past Taji at the top of the dome and struck the hole into space, sealing it instantly.

Xing-Xing leapt up from the gunner's seat, flapped her wings hard, and made for the apex. When Taji saw her coming, he let go of the beam he was clinging to. Xing-Xing caught him neatly, flipping him onto her back.

"Hold on tight!" she said.

"Oh, I'm gonna! Don't you worry!"

Xing-Xing nosedove with Taji hanging onto the straps to her wings—while behind and above them the dome was struck by a dozen new meteoroids puncturing holes in the super-thick glass and letting oxygen flood out. Taji could see below them that the dome was otherwise evacuated: they were the only ones left. They escaped by darting through the last open tubeway. Xing-Xing slapped the door's control lever as she flew past, sealing the tubeway behind them and closing off Central Dome for good.

From the command center atop the control tower, Deputy Olafsson was appraising the devastation through a hyperscope. He turned to Governor Tang to report:

"Sir, there's damage on every dome. Central Dome has been hit hardest."

"What about the air supply?" asked Mr. Barnett, thinking like an engineer.

"The oxygen processing station is housed in a bunker fifty feet beneath Central Dome," said the governor. "Only an atomic event could break it open. These aren't the bad old days when every diamond-prospector's hut needed its own cannister of O_2 for atmosphere. The system is centralized and secure."

"Sir!" called a technician. He was pointing to one of the smaller screens in the room. Its live feed of the West Landing Zone showed the tsunami of space-rocks striking the rocket-ships parked upright there. Rather than watch it electronically, everyone rushed to the glass walls of the orb to look out and see it with their own eyes.

They now beheld a sight so hideous that it was as if all their worst fears had been packed together into a single hyper-nightmare: rocket-ships were tumbling into one another like dominoes in slow motion, most exploding on impact. The Biarritz actually blasted off, its atomic engines having been triggered accidentally by an adjacent blast. It shot up high over the lunar surface; but pilot-less, it began to veer into an arc, then tipped over and headed back down.

Gaining velocity in descent, the rogue rocket crashed into Central Dome, its atomic engines roaring. From there it barreled straight into the grass covering the dome's floor, piercing the ground and penetrating multiple layers of rock and concrete. The rocket's nose cone broke through the roof of the bunker fifty feet down, the very bunker that housed the colony's oxygen processing station.

But *The Biarritz* didn't stop there. With its engines petering out though not yet dead, it drilled into the facility and nudged up against the oxygen processors and their connected pumps. A moment of calm followed in which it seemed that the situation might have stabilized. Then *The Biarritz* blew up.

The atomic detonation cracked open the dome above, sending the dome's contents twirling into space. Whole hillocks and long strips of the bike path, all the cutlery from the food court, bicycles, plastic wings, palm trees, lawn chairs, a thousand sushi rolls made for a wedding reception that was now going to have to be postponed, somebody's guitar, the bronze statues of Laika, Neil Armstrong, Sfiso Mahlobo, and Moonbeard Marc, the Space Gazelle Ice Cream sign from the soda shop, and ninety-six bags of frozen french fries were scattered to the stars: instant space-junk.

Up in the command center, still watching what was happening through a hyper-scope, Deputy Olafsson turned away from the shocking spectacle to consult a newly beeping monitor. Then he gave the governor the bad news:

"Sir, the oxygen processing station has been destroyed. Air circulation across Cosmopolis has ceased."

All eyes in the room turned to Governor Tang. The tension was supreme and the anticipation unbearable. With a grim voice, the governor declared:

"Canutus, inflate the space-raft and issue the order for total lunar evacuation. We have to get everyone off the Moon."

CHAPTER: 7

WITH GOVERNOR TANG'S ORDER for lunar evacuation in effect, colonists were hurrying through tubeways in an urgent though orderly fashion, on their way to the space-raft hangar. Xing-Xing and Taji, evacuating along with everyone else, spotted Mrs. Barnett up ahead—but she was rushing in the wrong direction: against traffic.

"Mom!"

"Taji!"

"Mom, you're going the wrong way!"

"Byron's still out on the surface! I need to get to the airlock!"

"Mrs. Barnett, I'm sure his class is being properly evacuated!" Xing-Xing said. "You have to come with us to the space-raft!"

"You and Taji go ahead—right now I need to get to the airlock and get outside!"

"Mrs. Barnett, please! At least let me take you up to the orb! They'll know where Byron is!"

Mrs. Barnett agreed. In her imagination she was picturing Byron stranded on the lunar surface, meteoroids exploding like bomblets all around him, boxing him in.

The reality was less distressing: Byron was inside a lunar cave near Rattlesnake Rill, laughing out loud as he and José Ignacio half-floated, half-fell toward the bottom of an inner abyss that they'd willingly jumped into. He was using his flashlight to scan the rock walls during this low-gravity descent of maybe a hundred feet. He felt like a balloon running low on helium: spinning, drifting, wafting to the ground.

It was an interesting coincidence that back at Cosmopolis, the lunar evacuation plan was also about to rely on the physics of low gravity as applied to human balloons of a sort. Inside the space-raft hangar, Deputy Olafsson threw a lever on the control board, causing a giant mass of superplastic to start inflating on the floor of this vast airlock. In a matter of minutes the raft resembled a colossal silver beach ball, its diameter several hundred feet, its globular body fitted with hundreds of clear plastic ovals for windows.

Once the inflation process was complete, Deputy Olafsson and six technicians pulled open the space-raft's dozens of portals. Colonists began climbing in, sealing themselves in their spacesuits as they went. On the inside, this superplastic beach ball was little more than a honeycombed webwork of nylon: a giant, no-frills escape pod, empty except for mesh seats and rigging to secure passengers in place at every possible angle to one another, in order to make full use of available space. In a matter of minutes colonists in the thousands were strapping themselves down for departure.

By this time Mrs. Barnett had reached the control tower with Xing-Xing and Taji. Her timing was both good and bad, because just when the elevator doors opened into the orb, she saw coming up on the big screen a fuzzy, black-and-white image of Miss Ahlooloo, transmitting from inside the lunar school bus on the regolith.

"Miss Ahlooloo!" barked Governor Tang into a microphone, "Why haven't you evacuated?!"

"The new boy's missing! He went over the ridge wall and down into the canyon! I can't find him!"

"Get the rest of the children back to Cosmopolis immediately!"

"Why are you *telling* her that?" Mr. Barnett said. "She can't leave without Byron!"

"She has to! There's no time!" Into the microphone the governor added: "Leave Byron the moon buggy, but you get out of there right now! Take the children directly to the space-raft!"

A lady's gasp behind them caused the governor, Mr. Barnett, and all the technicians in the command center to spin around. There stood Mrs. Barnett, beside Taji and Xing-Xing.

"He'll come back over the ridge and find the buggy!" Governor Tang said, to reassure Mrs. Barnett about Byron. "We'll stay here and watch for him until the last possible second! It's the best I can do!"

By now Byron and José Ignacio were exploring the inner abyss of their lunar cave, using Byron's flashlight to see by. They had just come to a fork in the rocky passage.

"*You go east,*" Byron said through his spacesuit intercom. "*I'll go west.*"

Boy and robot turned in the same direction, bumping into each other, Byron's nose jabbing a knob on José Ignacio's torso.

"*You go EAST I said!*"

"*I was!*"

"*No, you were not! THAT way's east. What's the MATTER with you?*"

"*All right! I didn't want to go alone! It's spooky down here! And dark!*"

"*So turn on some extra rotors!*"

Without waiting for José Ignacio to do it himself, Byron stood on his tiptoes and cranked a dial on José Ignacio's neck, causing various light-emitting mechanisms to start spinning inside the robot's transparent cranium, lighting his path in various colors.

"*Remember,*" Byron said, "*a real explorer can't find new oceans unless first he has the courage to lose sight of shore.*"

With a sigh, José Ignacio went off on his own, while Byron went in the opposite direction. He made his way through a tunnel of rock for about twenty feet before he saw something dead ahead that changed everything.

"*José Ignacio!*"

José Ignacio came flying back at top speed. He hovered beside Byron, staring in disbelief. Ahead of them was a thick curtain of green, leaf-bearing vines, completely blocking the tunnel.

"*Vegetation!*" Byron whispered.

"*But there's no atmosphere on the Moon,*" José Ignacio said. "*So how can there be flora?*"

"*I don't know the answer to that,*" Byron admitted, taking a step forward, "*but I'm gonna find out.*"

"*Wait! It might be toxic to the touch! It might be crawling with flesh-eating microbes! It might come alive and strangle you on contact! It might—*"

Byron grabbed José Ignacio by the claw and leapt at the vines, easily yanking the robot along, since he was already hovering on his jets in the low gravity.

They plunged together through the thick curtain of vines and exited the other side in a tumble. Standing up, they brushed themselves clean of stray leaves. Then Byron widened the angle on his flashlight, revealing a world of lush, blue-green vegetation. With only the flashlight to see by, it wasn't sufficiently bright to get a very clear view of things, but it was good enough. Byron could make out leaves and ferns, ivies and wildflowers, even a waterfall.

"Rabiznazibar!" he whispered, coining a new word for himself on the spot. *"It's some kinda whole sub-lunar ecosystem! José Ignacio, do you realize what this means? I'm not just an explorer anymore: I'm a discoverer!"*

With meteoroids still striking every dome in Cosmopolis, final preparations were underway to launch the space-raft and evacuate the colonists. Standing at the control console, Deputy Olafsson used the intercom to call Governor Tang, who was still with the Barnetts in the orb.

"Sir, we're ready to go on this end! What's your status?"

Governor Tang turned away from Deputy Olafsson's supersized face on the big screen and told the Barnetts:

"You have to get to the space-raft. Right now."

"I'm not leaving the Moon without my son," Mrs. Barnett said in quite a stern voice.

The governor looked to Mr. Barnett, hoping for a different answer; but Mr. Barnett said:

"I'm not leaving without my son and my wife."

"I'm not leaving without my parents and my brother," Taji added.

"And I'm not leaving without *you*, daddy," Xing-Xing said.

"Well, I'm not leaving until everyone else is safely away," Governor Tang stated firmly. He turned back to the screen and gave his orders:

"Deputy Olafsson, launch the space-raft. We're staying here."

"Yes, sir. Good luck to you, sir."

In the space-raft hangar, Deputy Olafsson unlocked a security box on the control console, then flipped the switch inside. This caused a timer on the console to begin clicking off a two-minute countdown. Deputy Olafsson placed his bubble-helmet on his head, sealed his spacesuit, dashed into the last open portal on the space-raft, and zipped it closed from the inside.

The hangar's domed roof curled open, and the space-raft rose up on a catapult resembling a gargantuan ball-chucker for a dog.

The timer on the console struck "zero"—and the catapult fired, flinging the colossal pod of superplastic away from the surface of the Moon and out into space. It spun as it went, faces of departing colonists visible all around its surface, peering out through plastic windows at a devastated Cosmopolis below, where precious air was still rushing out from hundreds of meteoroid-made holes in the city's domes and tubeways.

As the space-raft began its slow passage toward Earth, a distress signal emanated from its stubby antenna. The signal reached an outlying satellite and from there was redirected down to Banana Bread, Florida, where EarthCom was sure to pick it up.

Back in the orb, the Barnetts and Tangs watched the space-raft vanish from view. Mr. Barnett informed the Governor:

"I'm going out to find Byron."

"I'm going with you," Mrs. Barnett said.

"You don't know the moonscape," the governor reminded them both. "You'll lose your way."

"Be that as it may," said Mr. Barnett, "we're not leaving our child out there to fend for himself."

"*I'll* go," said the governor. "At least I know the terrain. You stay here and look after my daughter."

"Daddy?"

Everyone turned to Xing-Xing, then turned again to see what she was pointing at. On the horizon, the trajectory of an incoming meteoroid seemed as if it might bring the flying rock directly at them. They all held their breath ... clenched their teeth ... said their prayers ...

But the incoming meteoroid—as large as a house now—did not strike the tower. Instead it hit the regolith some fifty yards in *front* of the tower, smashing into a parked mooncrawler and sending the hefty machine flying. It was the mooncrawler itself which, banking off a boulder, slammed into the base of the control tower with terrible force, knocking it clean off its foundation. There was a jumble of shrieks and screams in the orb as the tower tumbled, rolled, slowed, wobbled ... and came to a stop.

"Is anyone hurt?!" Governor Tang said.

They were bruised and they were scraped, and Taji's elbow was cut, but otherwise they were okay. Unfortunately they were now in an orb on top of a tower lying on its side. With equipment torn from the walls and strewn in every direction, it was hard to move. Nevertheless, Xing-Xing managed to get to the emergency exit next to the damaged elevator. She jabbed its release button: the door's internal lock could be heard clicking open, but the door itself didn't budge.

"I think the emergency hatch is blocked from the other side!"

Taji climbed over a heap of metal to help out. He gave the emergency hatch a good kick, to no effect. "We're trapped," he said. "And there's no one left on the Moon to call for help."

"Unless ..." said Mr. Barnett, musing half out loud, half in his head.

Mrs. Barnett guessed what her husband was thinking.

"You made them to work both ways," she said.

"Made *what* to work both ways?" asked the governor.

"We're wearing ultrasound transponders," explained Mr. Barnett. "We can signal to Byron."

"Well, whatever we do," said Xing-Xing, examining the primary control panel that was now overturned on the floor, "we'd better do it fast. We're leaking air."

Mr. Barnett nodded to his wife and Taji. They all flipped open the crystal faces on their transponders and pressed their panic buttons. The buttons lit up, shooting ultrasonic waves out from the orb, across the wreckage of Cosmopolis, and over the surface of the Moon. Deep down in his sub-lunar cave, Byron would've seen the distress signal in a matter of seconds, but since he was wearing his own transponder on his wrist and his wrist was covered by his spacesuit, he saw nothing. He was focused anyway on the job at hand, using his flashlight to explore this underground cavern's plant life and waterfall.

"Do you think it's safe for me to take off my helmet?" he asked José Ignacio via intercom.

"Absolutely not!"

Byron unlatched his helmet, lifted it off his head, and took a deep breath while José Ignacio shook his cranium in disgust.

Suddenly Byron began choking on whatever exotic atmosphere he was breathing down here: he gulped and gasped, he fell to the ground, he thrust his hands over his head, his fingers awiggle. Then, with a little cough, he expired.

José Ignacio was unimpressed. *"You're no Alexander Fanta,"* he said, meaning that actor from the movies about the mutant panda bears.

Byron smiled with his eyes still closed, then jumped up

and declared:

"The air's fine!"

"Lucky for you."

"Ooh! I should collect a sample of the vegetation!"

He unlatched and removed the left-hand glove of his spacesuit to better pluck a leaf off a plant with his bare fingers. As he reached for the leaf, the sleeve of his undershirt slipped back, revealing the flashing transponder around his wrist. He turned to José Ignacio quizzically. *"You think it's broken?"* he said.

"Why would it be?"

"I think it's broken."

"Because … ?"

"Because we're in the middle of a major scientific discovery and I don't want to be interrupted? Obviously it's not working right: I didn't turn it on."

"But everyone else in your family is wearing a transponder too!"

"So?"

"So maybe your parents need YOUR help for once!"

Thanks to minimal gravity, Byron was able to rock-climb at high speed up the long shaft from the sub-lunar world back to the surface. He and José Ignacio then dashed out the mouth of the cave and scrambled up along the side of the canyon. But at the top of the ridge, they had an ugly surprise: Byron's class was gone. No kids, no teacher, no bus.

"Look!" said José Ignacio. He was pointing at the moon buggy, sitting there ready to go.

Also there, laid out in the shape of an arrow on the regolith right in front of the vehicle, was Honeybun's purple-and-gold sash, the one she'd taken off her sari in the airlock to wear over her spacesuit, the one that was so colorfully easy to see in the otherwise gray-and-white moonscape.

"That must be the way back!" José Ignacio said.

Never in his life had Byron been so happy to see a female fashion accessory, because he wasn't at all sure which way it was to Cosmopolis. Honeybun must've realized he'd be slightly disoriented, despite his otherwise excellent sense of direction—this being his very first time on the lunar surface. So she'd left him a marker. He made a mental note to give her a hearty handshake of thanks the next time he saw her. Assuming he lived through the day.

By now the Barnetts and Tangs had composed themselves on heaps of metal in the upended control tower: waiting, worrying, and breathing heavily, because their air was running out. The Barnetts' transponders, which had received no reply since they'd activated them, all at once began blinking green.

Mrs. Barnett gasped. "He's all right! Byron's all right!"

"Come on, Byron," said Mr. Barnett to himself, "show us what you're made of."

Byron was at this same moment speeding back toward Cosmopolis in the moon buggy, bouncing across the lunar surface, dodging meteoroid strikes and checking the three blinking dots on his transponder's hologram that indicated his family's location. The meteoroid strikes were nothing short of ferocious, but having zigzagged around incoming space-rocks many times in his imagination, most recently during The Incident Of The Missing Red Cape, Byron was perhaps better prepared than your average Lunarite to dodge the real thing shooting down onto the actual Moon.

"Watch out!" shouted José Ignacio, pointing at three different

meteoroids coming in from three different directions, but all heading toward the same spot: them.

Byron swerved hard to run the buggy up a lunar mound. This launched them off the surface, just high enough (about fifteen feet) to avoid becoming the filling in a meteoroid sandwich. The buggy spun three hundred and sixty degrees in mid "air," but by luck landed wheel-side-down, bouncing roughly before digging into the regolith and grabbing enough traction to shoot forward.

"Are you recording all this?" Byron said. *"I might want to refer to it later for professional purposes!"*

José Ignacio tapped a claw against his glass cranium, pointing to the array of lights inside. *"If the memory bulb is blinking, the robot is recording."*

Inside the toppled control tower, it was Xing-Xing's sharp eyes that first spotted the buggy weaving through the maze of Cosmopolis.

"I see him!"

Byron pulled up in the buggy, unbuckled himself, and ran to the tower, where he pressed his helmet to the glass orb. He could see his family even through the tint and started shouting at them, though of course inside the orb they couldn't hear him ... until Xing-Xing lay down on the floor beside the upside-down control panel—avoiding a sparking circuit threatening to light her sleeve on fire—and reached in to work a knob. "Got it!" she said.

Byron's voice via his spacesuit intercom came crackling over the speakers:

"... okay, mom! Are YOU okay?"

Xing-Xing yanked a microphone out from a mangled

mass of wires, handing it to Mrs. Barnett to use:

"We're all fine, sweetheart. Are you hurt anywhere?"

"Not that I know of!"

"What happened to you?"

"Well, the teacher said I could chase the daylight line, and then I mighta lost track of the time, because when I turned around to look for the rest of the class, they were already gone!"

Governor Tang took the microphone. "Byron, our emergency exit is blocked. We can't get out or even get to our spacesuits. We'll have to blast open the hatch, so we need you to bring back plasma grenades from the armory. There should be three of them in a vault inside the Miners' Dome, next to the diamond vault. I pointed it out to you on our tour this morning. Do you remember?"

"Yes!"

"Very good! There's only one problem. The armory's combination is twenty digits long. By any chance are you carrying a pad and pencil?"

"No! But I can remember it!"

"If you punch in the wrong numbers, the lock will automatically shut down for sixty minutes before letting you try again. It's a security precaution."

"That's okay—I'll wait around if I have to."

"Unfortunately, according to the oxometer in here, we only have twenty-four minutes of air left. So you'll only have one chance to get the numbers right. Are you sure you can remember it?"

"I have a secret system! Fire away!"

CHAPTER: 8

"*Your secret system is ME?!*" José Ignacio said.

"*Just keep repeating the numbers!*" Byron insisted.

"4266-2516-0005-1020-3757," droned José Ignacio. "4266-2516-0005-1020-3757."

They were in the moon buggy, speeding toward the Miner's Dome to retrieve from the armory vault the plasma grenades they needed to blast open the emergency hatch in the control tower and rescue everyone trapped inside. Byron had promised Governor Tang that he could remember the vault's twenty-digit combination, but getting it wrong even once would mean shutting down the automatic lock for an hour, and his parents and brother and the Tangs only had twenty minutes of air left to breathe.

In the tubeway to the Miner's Dome, Byron, still in his spacesuit, tore forward at his very fastest sprint, José Ignacio flying beside him while repeating a number that was turning out to be a challenge to keep straight, even for an automaton:

"4266-2516-0005-1020-3757."

Their concentration was so intense that it doubled the shock when, racing around a corner, they slammed into Lucky von Stroganoff running the other way. Byron and Lucky were both knocked to the ground in the collision. Byron jumped up first, yelling via intercom:

"*Golly!*"

"*Byron, what are you DOING in here! The Moon's supposed to be evacuated!*"

—"*Sssshhhh!*" José Ignacio threw his claws to his cranium and raised his voice to drown out the distraction, desperately trying to keep the numbers straight:

"4266-2516-0005-1020-3757!"

All Lucky saw was Byron wearing his toy robot on a cord around his neck, and Byron himself mumbling a long set of numbers. But from Byron's perspective, it was his full-sized robot repeating the combination. In any case, without explaining themselves Byron and José Ignacio darted away from Lucky, toward the armory vault, leaping over debris from the heavy meteoroid strikes that had hit this dome.

They reached the vault with Lucky trailing them, stomping his foot and demanding answers. Ignoring him, Byron punched the critical numbers into the keypad as José Ignacio called them out:

"4266-2516-0005-1020-3757."

Byron held his finger back from inputting the last four digits. *"Was it 3757 or 3727?"* he said.

"I'm not sure," José Ignacio admitted. *"I might've mixed myself up."*

Byron turned to Lucky. *"Which do you think?*

"Well, I prefer 3727."

Byron punched in "3757." The mechanism clicked, the vault slid open.

"How very insulting," Lucky huffed. *"Why ask my advice if you're going to ignore it?"*

"But you told me the wrong number!"

"Switching topics, I ask again: what are you doing here?"

"My family's trapped in the control tower. They sent me to get plasma grenades to blast 'em out. What are YOU doing here?"

"I'm collecting my diamonds. Or trying to. But I couldn't get into the jewelry vault. I was looking for some sort of explosive device when you ran into me."

Just now Byron spotted the plasma grenades that he was after, on a shelf between spare goo-gun parts. Reaching for them, he asked Lucky:

"*You stayed on the Moon for your diamonds? Are they really that important?*"

"*I already paid for them! If I leave them here, I'll bankrupt Papa's company! I don't dare go back to Earth empty-handed! Besides which, these could be the last diamonds off the Moon for years! If I do get them home, Papa will HAVE to forgive me. He may even start liking me again!*" Eyeing the plasma grenades that Byron was gently inserting into his spacesuit pockets, Lucky added: "*I don't suppose you could spare one of those to help me out.*"

"*That's not in my mission statement.*"

Lucky put on a brave face, but Byron could tell he was hurt.

"*Right,*" said Lucky. "*I understand. Not a problem. You go save your family. I'll stay here and try to think of another way to save mine.*"

"*Oh, all right! But we have to hurry!*"

Lucky scurried out of the room and over to the adjacent diamond vault, Byron running behind him. What followed was an exceedingly speedy operation: one plasma grenade and one detonation later, Lucky was inside the vault looking for his jewels.

"*Just take YOUR diamonds!*" Byron called in after him. "*Nobody else's!*"

"*Do you mistake me for a cat burglar?*" Lucky called back. "*Of COURSE I'm only taking mine!*"

"*Okay, but speed it up! We gotta move!*"

"*Found them!*"

"*Then let's go!*"

A minute and forty seconds later, they were bouncing violently in the moon buggy on their way to the orb, Lucky in the back seat holding tight to his case of diamonds. "*Slow down!*" he said. "*You're making me sick!*"

Byron took the next curve at high speed.

"*I'm retching!*" Lucky warned.

"*Do not throw up in my vehicle!*" Byron ordered, stepping on the accelerator.

Lucky made a strange sound: half gurgling, half gargling; then, indeed, he vomited. His puke was the color of the inside of an avocado. Fortunately his bubble helmet contained it.

"*How foul!*" José Ignacio whispered to Byron, keeping his voice low so he wouldn't make Lucky feel worse.

From inside the wreck of the toppled control tower, Mr. Barnett spotted Byron's moon buggy weaving back through the ruins of the lunar city.

"There he is!"

Byron pulled up and jumped out, while Lucky stayed in the vehicle, jerking his head back and forth to try to knock the vomit away from that part of his helmet directly in front of his eyes. But this only slid the vomit around his helmet even more, until he could almost not see out at all and had to sit still in the buggy, blinded by his own throw-up.

"*I got the grenades!*" Byron shouted via intercom as he ran up to the orb and peered through the glass at his parents inside.

"*Good work, Byron!*" said Governor Tang. "*Now listen to me very closely. Here's what you have to do next ...*"

Ninety seconds later, in the access shaft at the bottom of the tower, Byron pulled himself toward the command center, following the governor's instructions. The low gravity helped him along, but the shaft was dangerously narrow. Behind him, in single-file due to the tight space, came José Ignacio, moving along via tiny bursts out of his boot jets. Meanwhile, in the orb itself, fiddling at the upside-down control panel, Xing-Xing said:

"I've got the cameras working!"

Though the big screen was upside-down too, by tilting their heads the trapped group could now watch Byron, in black-and-white, moving through the access shaft. Governor Tang communicated with him using the microphone to the tower's PA system, which also transmitted to all spacesuit intercoms within range.

"You're doing fine, Byron. That's the airlock's emergency hatch right in front of you. Just twist the knob to open it."

Inside the access shaft, Byron looked back over his shoulder to ask José Ignacio:

"Which way do I twist?"

"Righty tighty, lefty loosey. Just because we're on the Moon doesn't mean we've left common sense behind."

Byron worked the knob as advised—and the hatch opened to the sound of air whooshing out. Pulling himself in, Byron sealed the hatch behind him, to keep the rest of the oxygen from escaping. Then he turned around and surveyed the scene: up ahead he saw a mass of mangled metal blocking his way. Also visible, near the far hatch into the orb itself, was a rack of spacesuits.

"Governor Tang, it's all blocked up! I can't get to your side!"

Watching him on-screen, the Tangs and Barnetts could see the mass of metal blocking Byron's way. They also saw Byron's toy robot, attached to his belt as usual, by cord.

"Byron, all you have to do is pull the pin on a plasma grenade and get it to our end of the airlock, to blow open our hatch. Do you see any clear path at all?"

Byron managed to locate a clear path, maybe eighteen inches high, on a flat stretch of what had become the shaft's "floor."

"Yes! I see a path!"

"Good! Put the grenade in your robot's arms and send it through!"

" 'It?' " sniffed José Ignacio. "He can't be referring to ME."

Byron was less offended than José Ignacio, though equally confused. "But José Ignacio can't get through there! He's over seven feet tall!"

Looking mystified, and a bit alarmed, the governor turned to Byron's parents. Mr. Barnett reached for the microphone.

"Byron Benedicto Timoteo Valiente Barnett, this is no time for tomfoolery! Your robot stands twelve inches off the ground! If you switch him on, he can walk to our side carrying the grenade! So by the count of ten that robot had better be armed and marching! One ... two ..."

In the access shaft Byron was listening to his father uneasily:

" ... three ... four ... "

Byron gave the seven-foot José Ignacio behind him a rare glance of sympathy. He knew that even if the robot could somehow force his way through the mass of metal ahead to deliver the plasma grenade to the blocked hatch, he wouldn't be able to make his way back before the grenade went off.

" ... six ... seven ... "

Byron pulled the pin out of the first of the two remaining grenades, but still hesitated.

In the command center Mr. Barnett was slowing down as he counted out: " ... ... eight ... ... nine ... ..."

"I see it!" Taji said.

On-screen the little toy robot was marching through the narrow passage, carrying the ticking plasma grenade in its outstretched arms. When it reached the far side of the passage and bumped into the blocked emergency hatch, a long cord attached to its leg was yanked delicately, knocking it over and releasing the grenade, which nestled against the hatch. Then the toy robot was yanked back hard and fast in Byron's direction.

Byron jumped out of the access shaft as instructed, pulling the toy robot on its cord behind him. He slammed and sealed the shaft's outer door. Not six seconds later the plasma grenade detonated inside the shaft—and the emergency hatch blew apart.

Out on the lunar surface again, Byron stood before the seven-foot-and-several-centimeters José Ignacio, a thirteen-inch-tall panel open on the robot's flank, a panel which until this very minute Byron had always thought was just a metal seam. Byron detached the *toy* robot from its long cord, slotted it back inside the full-scale José Ignacio, and watched the panel close up to contain it. Then he asked José Ignacio:

"Why didn't you ever tell me you kept a sub-unit on hand for micro-operations?"

"Even a robot is entitled to a modicum of privacy."

The outer hatch to the tower now opened from the inside, and out came everybody, all wearing spacesuits.

"Byron!" shouted Mrs. Barnett. She pulled him in and hugged him hard, after which Mr. Barnett did the same. Taji grabbed his little brother by the neck and shook him affectionately.

"Great job, Boon!"

"Byron, that was true derring-do," said Governor Tang.

Xing-Xing offered her own words of appreciation while slotting a fresh oxygen-cartridge into Byron's spacesuit, then she stepped over to the moon buggy and repeated the procedure for Lucky. After that she explained to the group:

"*Those were the last two oxygen-cartridges from the control tower. Now we've all got four hours of air: more than enough to get where we're going.*"

"*Which is where?*" asked Mr. Barnett. It was the governor who answered:

"*To the edge of Crater Copernicus. Governor Mahlobo built a weekend lodge there. It's the last of the old pre-dome structures, so it uses canistered oxygen, which we keep well-stocked. Also there's a space-radio we can signal our location from, to alert the rescue-rocket.*"

"*Rescue-rocket?*" said Byron.

"*That's right. We have to get off the Moon as fast as we can.*"

"*Get OFF the Moon? But I just got ON the Moon!*"

"*And I'm afraid you'll be the last boy to set foot here for quite some time.*"

Soon the lunar school bus was a tiny, shiny square crossing a rounded stretch of moonscape, passing between craters the size of small cities back on Earth. Governor Tang was at the wheel. Behind him, Mr. and Mrs. Barnett shared a seat, Mr. Barnett squeezing his wife's spacesuit-gloved hand. Behind Mr. and Mrs. Barnett sat Taji and Xing-Xing. Behind Taji and Xing-Xing, Lucky von Stroganoff sat alone. The vomit inside his bubble-helmet had dried by now, so he couldn't see out at all, and no one could see in.

At the rear of the bus Byron and José Ignacio sat together, both gazing in fascination at a lunar mountain range, watching the Earth sink behind it and mesmerized by the spectacular disaster of meteoroids still peppering Cosmopolis in the distance.

"*Boy versus Nature, José Ignacio. See what I mean? Cause ya never know what Nature's gonna do next.*"

It wasn't much longer before the bus, rolling across the regolith, came within sight of what was very possibly the Moon's most beautiful indentation: Crater Copernicus, after the famed Polish astronomer, Nicolaus Copernicus, born five hundred years earlier and still a big name in the space biz. At the edge of it Byron spotted the weekend lodge built by another eminent individual: Sfiso Mahlobo, first head of the Lunar League and first Governor of the Moon.

So this vehicle carrying the remaining population of the Moon, "Cosmopolites" in the morning but refugees since right before lunch, made its way toward a safe haven beside one of the Moon's greatest craters. Never in the history of human doings had a safe haven been needed more than right now. With the glass walls of the lodge sparkling in the starlight, the bus pulled up, its passengers all deeply relieved to be here, though more than a little nervous about what would happen next.

CHAPTER: 9

THE REFUGEES FROM COSMOPOLIS entered the old glass lodge on the edge of Crater Copernicus. Governor Tang led the way into the airlock, then came Mr. and Mrs. Barnett, then Xing-Xing and Taji, then Byron leading Lucky—who couldn't see due to the dried vomit inside his helmet.

Once indoors, the governor's first order of business was firing up the early-model atomic generator: this brought up the lights and revealed the lodge to be surprisingly cozy in décor, not unlike a ski lodge at the top of an alp.

Next the governor worked the main valve on a row of interlinked oxygen canisters, flooding the room with breathable air; and after that he touched a button beside the stone fireplace, which started up a gas flame and contributed to the room's comfy ambience.

Soon the wall-mounted oxometer blinked green, signaling that helmets could be safely removed. This meant the most to Lucky, who could now separate himself from the puke that had dried inside his helmet and blinded him during the trip here. He was still feeling faintly queasy from being subjected to Byron's high-speed driving in the moon buggy, but at least the urge to heave had eased off. So he sat himself down in a wingback chair by the fireplace to calm his nerves while his traveling companions explored the lodge's facilities ...

Mrs. Barnett went directly into the kitchen where she found stores of vacuum-sealed food in metallic packets. Xing-Xing went to examine a rack of rifle-sized goo guns, each with the distinctive corkscrew barrel; and the governor was already fiddling at the old space-radio. Before long he found the right frequency. Everyone else stopped what they were doing to listen as he spoke into the microphone:

"Come in, EarthCom, this is Governor Tang of the Lunar League, transmitting from the Moon."

He waited a moment, then tried it again:

"EarthCom, come in. This is Governor Jing Tang of the Lunar League transmitting a Priority Alpha distress message from the Moon."

What followed was a hideous silence of twelve seconds during which it seemed that the space-radio might not be working, meaning the Tangs, the Barnetts, and the von Stroganoff would not be able to call for help and might never be heard from again. Then a voice crackled through the small speaker:

"This is EarthCom. We read you, Mr. Governor."

"EarthCom, thank goodness!"

"Sorry about that delay. We're in the middle of an electrical storm down here in Banana Bread and it's scrambling our circuits. We had to switch over to a relay via Australia to get our signal back up to you."

"Understood, EarthCom. "

"Mr. Governor, what is your status?"

"We're a group of seven persons stranded outside Cosmopolis. I'm requesting a rescue-rocket for emergency evacuation."

"Roger that. We have several rescue-rockets presently deployed in Earth orbit—the flagship is under the command of Admiral Haddad herself. Patching you through now."

Fleet Admiral Zahra Haddad, whose previous job had been head of the Middle Eastern Air Force, now wore the violet uniform of the Astral Corps, of which she was the top officer. At the moment though she wasn't on the bridge of her ship, she was in its massive cargo hold, helping evacuees from the Moon cross over from their space-raft through a transfer tube. The captains of half a dozen other rescue-rockets were doing likewise nearby, emptying the space-raft of its thousands of passengers.

Together with Deputy Olafsson, Admiral Haddad had just given a hand to an elderly lunar lady who was having trouble with the last step out of the transfer tube when an aide appeared carrying a portable transceiver and explaining who was on the line. The admiral immediately shifted her attention over to this new matter, stepping away with Deputy Olafsson and speaking into the device:

"Governor Tang, this is Admiral Haddad on the line. What a relief to know you're alive!"

"*The relief is all mine, Admiral Haddad. So what's your schedule looking like? Any chance you can fit in a rescue operation? We're at the old Governor's Lodge at the edge of Crater Copernicus.*"

The admiral turned to Deputy Olafsson, who confirmed:

"I know the spot."

"Roger that, Mr. Governor," said the admiral. "We're just collecting the evacuees from your space-raft now. But I'm afraid this barrage of meteoroids is going to block us from reaching the Moon for another ten or twelve hours. How's your oxygen supply looking? Can you wait out the day if need be?"

"*We have air to breathe all weekend.*"

"Excellent. We'll get to you the minute it's clear. Signing off for now."

Governor Tang replaced the radio's microphone on its hook and told his fellow refugees:

"Now we wait."

"Is anyone else peckish?" Lucky called over from his chair by the fireplace. "I'm in the mood for a nibble."

"*I'm* peckish," Byron agreed, shooting his hand up.

"I think we could all use a nice hot meal," Mrs. Barnett said. She stepped into the kitchen again, telling the group: "Everyone just relax for half an hour and then we'll eat."

With his mother busy whipping up a meal, Taji intended to spend the free time with Xing-Xing. He joined her on the love seat by the fireplace where she was warming her hands.

"So, Xing-Xing, back in the big dome you stopped me from being sucked into space by firing that goo-gun. You know what *that* means."

"Um, you're welcome?"

"It means you *have* to go out with me now."

"*Really?* And why is that?"

"Well, what's the point of saving my life if you're not gonna make the rest of the life you saved me for worth living?"

"Taji, your logic is never easy to follow."

"All right, all right! You drive a hard bargain, but yes! I'll give you another kiss to help you make up your mind about me!"

Xing-Xing tried hard not to smile, but she couldn't stop herself and broke out in a beautiful little laugh. Then she let Taji kiss her. Afterwards he said:

"That's absolutely the *last* freebie you're getting out of me! Now decide!"

"Don't you think we have bigger problems to solve right now than whether or not I'm going on a date with you?"

"Like I always say: if you take care of your love life, everything else falls into place."

Their chitchat, the stuff of a budding romance, continued in this vein for several minutes, while nearby Mr. and Mrs. Barnett, who were setting the table together, found themselves further down the line of love.

"Are you sorry you married me?" Mr. Barnett said.

"Wallace! How could you ever *think* such a thing?"

"Well ... I *am* the man who dragged you to the Moon just in time for the worst natural disaster in the history of the solar system."

"No one's dead and no one's hurt. The rescue-rocket is coming and we have plenty of oxygen to last until it gets here. We'll be fine."

"Then again, if you hadn't married me, you could've had your *own* life of personal fame and fortune."

Mrs. Barnett set down her stack of plates, circled around to her husband on the opposite side of the table, and placed her hands on both his cheeks. "My family *is* my fortune," she said. "I knew just what I wanted and I settled for nothing less. Now shut up and kiss me."

Mr. Barnett pulled her in for a kiss; then he hugged her, giving her a really good squeeze.

"Too tight?" he asked in mid-hug.

"Never," she whispered.

Around this time Byron found himself in the mood for a spot of conversation. But José Ignacio had plugged his power cord into an outlet on the lodge's antiquated atomic generator for a recharge and wasn't in a conversational modality, so Byron was forced to look around for someone else to shoot the breeze with ...

Taji was flirting with Xing-Xing on a love seat, so he was out of the running. Byron's parents were busy in the kitchen fixing lunch. Governor Tang might've been good for a bit of banter, but he was in the library nook going through the book collection. Which left only Lucky. He was sitting by a picture window, cleaning the puke out of his helmet. Byron ambled over and sat down beside him.

"I wish we had appetizers," Lucky said. "I'm not sure I can last until lunch."

Byron remembered the half a Space Cake in his belt buckle. He turned away from Lucky, slid open the buckle's secret compartment, extracted the Cake still in its foil wrapper, turned back to Lucky, and offered it up. "Venusian Vanilla," he said.

"Are you sure? You're hungry too."

"Your stomach's emptier. I can wait."

Lucky accepted the half a treat with a grateful nod. "Very kind of you," he said.

The truth was: Byron was good at sharing, even when snacks were involved. José Ignacio himself, who would happily give you a complete list of Byron's character flaws if asked, would also, if pressed, admit that Byron was, on the plus side of things, surprisingly generous.

With Lucky nibbling the Space Cake, Byron turned away again, this time to look out the window. Sunlight was blasting the floor of Crater Copernicus like a silver spotlight running at a million mega-volts. "Zanzibar!" he murmured, deeply moved by the splendor of this epic dimple on the Moon.

Lucky finished his snack, licked a vanilla crumb off his lips, and gave Byron the once-over. "I like the cobalt-blue," he said, meaning Byron's hair.

"*Thank* you! *Finally*! *Some*one who knows the difference between royal blue and *co*balt blue!"

"In fact," Lucky observed, "your hair has a sheen not unlike that of the cobalt-blue tarantula. You don't find that on too many heads."

Byron's mouth popped open in shock. No one else had *ever* made the connection between his signature hair color and the sheen of his favorite member of the spider family. He had to always *tell* people. And even then they frequently didn't get it. Until now. Lucky may've had a vomiting problem, but he clearly wasn't all bad.

"And I suppose I should thank you too," Lucky said, "for helping me save my diamonds. And for saving me from the wrath of Papa."

"Don't mention it."

They sat in silence for a moment, Lucky wiping out his helmet, Byron gazing at Crater Copernicus. Then Byron asked:

"Why do you say 'Pa-PAH' instead of PAH-pa?"

"That's just the way I pronounce it."

"Well, why's he so mad at you anyway? I mean, how bad *were* you?"

"Bad."

"What'd you do?"

Lucky took a big breath and exhaled musically. "I told you that Papa is a gem dealer and diamond-cutter. Well, I was a diamond-cutter-in-training. It takes years of practice to be able to put a mallet to a rough stone and whack it right."

"And you whacked it wrong?"

"Byron, how good is your imagination?"

"Good."

"Then let me set the scene for you. I'd been out cavorting with friends, and we'd drunk one round too many of coconut schnapps ..."

(In Byron's brain a picture flared of Lucky & Company stumbling out the door of a tavern in London, England, dressed like musketeers, wearing velvet top hats with feathers sewn onto the sides and drinking alcoholic beverages out of real coconuts, through swirly straws.)

"... and somehow the idea popped into my head that the perfect way to end the evening would be to show off my diamond-cutting skills."

Byron pictured Big Ben chiming midnight. In his mind's eye he flew up the side of the famous clock tower, then in through a window near the top. This, he imagined, was where Lucky lived. On the inside it was half Arabian tent, half safari tent, decorated with crazy carpets on the floor *and* hanging on the walls. Plus Lucky's pet was a baby leopard.

"So in my state of extreme tiddliness," Lucky said, "I took a hugely valuable stone out of Papa's vault, sat my friends down to watch, raised my mallet ... and turned a million-credit diamond into a mound of diamond dust."

"Ooh, that *is* bad," Byron admitted, scrunching his face. "You know what, you really don't have the right name for a person with your track record. Instead of Lucky von Stroganoff, maybe you could change it to—

"Barfy von Puke-A-Lot?" José Ignacio offered from his seat by the atomic generator. Byron turned to glare at the robot, though Lucky, following Byron's gaze, saw only the little toy robot on a chair across the room.

"Pukey von Throw-It-Up?" José Ignacio continued. "Hurly von Spew-A-Chunk?"

Byron shook his head at the robot's juvenile humor and turned back to Lucky.

"What I mean is, you need a whole new name to give you a whole new attitude. Something like ... 'Rodrigo Dragonsmasher.' "

"I've heard worse."

"Well, think about it."

"I will."

"So what happened after you broke the diamond?"

"Papa demoted me to errand boy. I've been picking up packages ever since." He reached for his case of diamonds. "So you see why I couldn't lose these: it would've been the end of me." He opened the case and showed Byron an array of gemstones glittering in their velvet bed.

José Ignacio piped up from across the room:

"I've never understood why humans go gaga over diamonds in the first place. They're just carbon atoms bonded together in a tetrahedral lattice. Big deal."

"How rude!" Byron shot back. "Mr. von Stroganoff is in the diamond *business*. You can't insult people's jobs! And for your information, humans love diamonds because they're sparkly and look great on turbans and belt buckles! Something you wouldn't understand because you're an overgrown transistor who doesn't wear clothes!"

Byron turned to Lucky and apologized: "Please excuse José Ignacio, he's not the politest robot ever built. Especially being over seven feet tall, he's very conceited. He loves the sound of his own voice. Basically he's a glorified circuit-board with a loudspeaker and a voltage ray. But I'm sorta stuck with him."

Lucky glanced again at the twelve-inch toy robot on its chair—and grasped the situation. "Yes," he commiserated, "robots do sometimes have a mind of their own. I entirely understand."

Byron called over to José Ignacio: "See? Those are called *good* manners. Try learning some!"

"How did you two end up together?" Lucky said.

"Well, that *is* a kinda funny story."

"I'm all ears."

"Okay, so it was my birthday last year. I was turning nine. And for a present I'd asked my parents if I could have a robot to help me out in my research."

"Sorry, what research is that?"

"Oh, you know: interdimensional phenomena, dinosaur bones, poltergeists, bubonic plague."

"Of course."

"So after my birthday dinner, I blew out the candles on my cake—

"What kind?"

"Devil's food with root-beer icing."

"Toppings?"

"Silver sprinkles and maraschino cherries. Plus a graham-cracker spoon to eat it with."

"Right. Go on."

"So I blew out the candles and then my parents said my present was in my father's study, where they'd been keeping it because I'm not allowed to go in there without permission and they know I like to sorta snoop around the house whenever there's a gift-giving situation coming up."

"Who doesn't?"

"So I ran into the study—and there was a crate, eight feet high, waiting for me with a crowbar to open it. Which I did. And inside was José Ignacio. All seven feet and several centimeters of his titanium corpus and golden switches."

As Byron described meeting his robot for the first time, Lucky realized that in all likelihood what had been waiting in Mr. Barnett's study was not an eight-foot crate but a nicely wrapped, normal-sized gift box containing the twelve-inch toy robot that was usually hooked to Byron's belt; but Lucky seemed to appreciate Byron's story anyway, even with all the embellishments.

"So I switched him on and introduced myself," Byron said.

Lucky folded his legs into his lap and made himself comfortable in his chair to listen to Byron recap that first conversation between himself and his robot. Here's how it went:

"Welcome to the Booniverse!" Byron said.

"Sorry, what did you say?"

"Wel-come ... to ... the ... *Boo*-niverse," Byron repeated slowly, thinking that José Ignacio must need a minute for his audio receptors to ramp up to full speed.

"I apologize for asking," the robot said, "but are you trying to say '*u*niverse'? Because I keep hearing a 'b' that doesn't belong there."

"No, it's right. The Booniverse."

"The *u*niverse."

"The *Boo*niverse."

"Pardon me," José Ignacio said, "I believe I'm detecting something in the way of a slight speech impediment. Not that that's anything to be ashamed of: many of the greatest beings in history have had speech impediments. I once knew a robot with a glitch in his programming that made him mix up the sounds in any number of words. So 'potato' came out 'toe-tay-poe' and 'joystick' 'stoy-jick.' Instead of 'chocolate ice cream' he'd say 'ock-o-lit chice-cream' ... and for 'quantum computer' you'd get 'cuantum qomputer,' though you couldn't really tell the difference on that one. Anyway, he went on to an illustrious career as a molecular nanotechnologist with no problem whatsoever. So you might even consider it a mark of distinction to—

"I don't have a speech impediment! I'm Byron 'Boon' Barnett and I live in the Booniverse! Which is where you live now too!"

"Uh-oh," said José Ignacio, wondering what was happening here.

Byron shook off his irritation, forced himself to smile, and started over:

"So. As mentioned, my name is Byron Barnett. Known to friends and admirers as Boon. Also known as Master of the Secret Canyon, Nomad in the Ninth Dimension, Steward of the Laser-Dagger, Patron of the Arts Ballistic, Keeper of the Golden Eyeball, Knight Commander of the Order of the Double Quasar, and Envoy Plenipotentiary to the Eleven Deadly Realms."

"Charmed," said José Ignacio, though in fact he was whatever the opposite of charmed was.

"Now what are we gonna call *you?*" Byron said.

"Uh ... my name? Which is Zeta-Bitonal-Dyna-Bot, Model 933, Lot 14, Production Cycle: Delta Echo Foxtrot Zulu Lima-Bean, Serial Number 04-12-19-66."

"Or we could go with ... 'José Ignacio.' "

"I beg your pardon?"

"José Ignacio—it's my uncle on my mom's side's name. José Ignacio Barcelona Bolaños. You sorta look like him."

"Or ... we could go with *my* name."

"Wait! I have a better idea! We'll call you 'ZBDB'! It's your initials. Zeta-Bitonal-Dyna-Bot. ZBDB! It's perfect!"

The robot sighed. "I'll take José Ignacio," he said.

"Good choice. So. Ready to get started?"

"Just one thing: could you *define* the 'Booniverse' for me? Just so we're on the same wavelength?"

"Let me put it like this: most people look at the cosmos and say: 'Oh, my gosh!' But *I* look at the cosmos and say: 'I can *fix* that!' "

"Uh-huh."

"José Ignacio, we have a lot of work to do. You showed up just in time."

"You know what? I'm thinking there's been some sort of miscommunication here. I actually requested a bookish-type person, somebody between the ages of sixty and eighty with a love of lying in bed reading long Russian novels. I'm more of a relax-around-the-house-type individual myself who's not looking to do too much wandering in the ninth dimension or cosmos-repair of any particular degree of difficulty."

"What do you mean, *you* requested?" Byron said, both confused and somewhat annoyed. "I requested *you*. You're my *birth*day present."

"Oh. Wow. That is so carbon-based-life-form of you, thinking about everything from *your* perspective. No appreciation at all that I come not just from a robot factory but a robot *community*. And that we get to request who we're shipped *out* to just like you get to request who you want shipped *in*. The paperwork that *I* filled out made it crystal clear that I was interested in a stay-at-home-type assignment that would be light on legwork and generous on catnaps. This is a two-year lease: can you imagine the nightmare of being paired up with the wrong partner that long? So I have to be candid with you: I don't see this working out and I'm urging you to crate me back up, send me straight back, and request an exchange."

"But I scheduled an expedition to By George Gorge for tomorrow! A whole day of digging for buried Spanish treasure! We could come back with a thousand gold coins—or at least a couple dozen ingots! I can't haul all that metal alone! That's why I put it on the calendar for the day after you got here, I've been planning it for months! It's my ninth birthday present to my*self*!"

"But surely you realize that if you switch me into main mode, your contract kicks in and the two-year clock starts ticking on my lease! After that, we're *stuck* with each other!"

"Well, then, we're just gonna have to make it work. The gold in By George Gorge isn't gonna dig itself, and tomorrow is our one day to get there and drill into the dirt! Anyway, I'm sure we can adjust to each other once we learn our likes and dislikes."

At this point in his story, Byron admitted to Lucky: "I mighta been wrong about that part."

And just then Mrs. Barnett sang out:

"*Lunch*-time!"

Byron abandoned his seat and zipped across the room to the table, where his mother was setting down a steaming tureen.

"I hope everybody likes butternut squash soup, cheese soufflé, and hot Parker House rolls," she said as the rest of the group took their seats. "It's the best I could manage on short notice."

Her modesty notwithstanding, Mrs. Barnett had produced something of a feast. Everyone dug in with the kind of hearty appetites that only escaping certain death can work up in you. Xing-Xing was the first to compliment the chef:

"Mrs. Barnett, this may be the most delicious meal I've ever eaten!"

"Really, mom!" Byron chimed in. "And not only cause we're so hungry!"

Even Lucky raved:

"Mrs. Barnett, this soufflé is a minor masterpiece! How ever did you do it with freeze-dried foodstuffs?"

"Bianca's a Renaissance woman," said Mr. Barnett. "She can do anything."

Byron now caught a glimpse of Governor Tang, seated at the far end of the table, staring right back at him. José Ignacio warned in a whisper:

"He's giving you the evil eye."

"No, he isn't," Byron whispered back. "I saved his life!"

"Right after you almost killed him by making him sit through a white worm attack because you were AWOL in a cave!"

"He doesn't even know about the cave! Don't bring it up!"

"Byron, I have a question for you," the governor said. Everyone else at the table stopped speaking to hear what it was. "When you said you were chasing the daylight line and lost track of the time, were you within sight of your class?"

Mr. Barnett interjected politely:

"Mr. Governor, I'm sure during his first hour on the surface of the Moon, Byron was careful enough not to stray from the group."

Governor Tang nodded. Then:

"It's just I still don't see how Miss Ahlooloo, who knows the terrain like the back of her hand, lost track of Byron."

"Well," Byron conceded with a nervous giggle, "maybe I was doing a *little* extra exploring."

"What do you mean, 'extra'?" Mr. Barnett said.

With great reluctance, Byron admitted: "Well ... as I recall, I was at the top of a cliff ... and at the bottom there was a canyon ... and in the canyon I could see ... a cave."

"Byron!" exclaimed Mrs. Barnett.

"We were on a field trip! I was trying to scoop up as much education out in the field as I could get my hands on!"

With Byron soon defending himself against a round of increasingly tough questioning, it was Xing-Xing who first noticed the danger. Glancing out through the glass walls of the lodge she became aware of very small meteoroid strikes in the distance. It took a second or two to register on her conscious mind, then she jumped up from the table hollering:

"Spacesuits!!!"

The group turned to see another mob of meteoroids shooting down from space—and coming their way. The debate on Byron's guilt or innocence instantly ceased as everyone jumped from the table and ran for their spacesuits.

"Where's my helmet?" shouted Lucky in terror. "I can't find my *helmet!*"

Xing-Xing took charge of the situation:

"Byron, you help Mr. von Stroganoff find his helmet! Taji, you grab two goo-guns!"

"But we can't shoot down meteoroids with *goo!*"

"Just get the guns and follow me!"

Taji grabbed two rifle-sized goo-guns off their rack. Then he and Xing-Xing suited up fast and dashed outside, guns in hand.

"If you hold onto the trigger, the goo keeps coming," Xing-Xing explained via spacesuit-intercom. *"Watch!"*

She fired her corkscrew-shaped rifle at an incoming meteoroid that was heading straight for the lodge. As long as she kept her finger on the trigger without letting go, the goo kept shooting in a long, purple strand. Once it struck and stuck to the meteoroid in question, it was as if Xing-Xing had lassoed the incoming space-rock and was still holding tight to her end of the rope. She dug her spacesuited heels into the regolith, tugging at the long length of goo connected to the meteoroid, grunting:

"Aaaaaaaaahhhhhhh!"

She pulled the meteoroid off its trajectory, swinging it down into the vastness of Crater Copernicus below. By combination of brain and brawn, Xing-Xing thus saved the lodge and everyone inside. She didn't have long to feel good about it. *"The bus!"* she hollered.

Taji swung around and spotted a meteoroid heading straight for the lunar school bus. Following Xing-Xing's example, he fired his goo-gun, hit the meteoroid—though not quite so squarely as Xing-Xing had hit hers—and pulled it off-course until it smashed into a ridge.

Inside the lodge, the Barnetts and Governor Tang had a dramatic view through the living room window of meteoroids coming down everywhere, and of Xing-Xing and Taji bravely defending them with goo. But they couldn't run out to help because they were now all looking for Lucky's missing helmet. If a meteoroid were to puncture a wall of the lodge, without his helmet on Lucky would suffocate in seconds.

"Found it!" Byron hollered via intercom—since he, his parents, and the governor were already suited up and wearing *their* helmets. *"It musta rolled behind the chair!"*

Outside, Xing-Xing had just fired at a particularly monstrous meteoroid and was straining with all her might to swing it away.

"Taji, grab hold of me!"

"I'm always good for a little fun, Xing-Xing, but do you really think now's the right time?"

"This rock's too big! Grab hold of me from behind and swing me around!"

Taji planted his feet firmly behind Xing-Xing, put his arms around her, and, pulling hard against the force of the incoming meteoroid on the other end of the goo-line, helped Xing-Xing swing the thing off course. Together they saved the lodge from instant annihilation, this time just as the rest of the group came running out of the airlock.

"Everyone into the bus!" ordered the governor.

They hurried into the vehicle, a throng of meteoroids slamming into the lodge behind them with such force that the structure was knocked right off its foundation. It tumbled into Crater Copernicus, flipped over as it fell, and crashed wrong-side-up on the crater floor below, bursting into flames on the inside before its glass walls blew out and the fire was extinguished by the loss of oxygen into the vacuum of the Moon.

CHAPTER: 10

GOVERNOR TANG WAS AGAIN behind the wheel of the lunar school bus, zigzagging as best he could to avoid the latest spate of meteoroids. Minutes earlier the refugees had abandoned the glass lodge they had taken shelter in beside Crater Copernicus, only moments before meteoroids destroyed the old abode by knocking it over the crater's edge.

The governor pressed his foot hard on the accelerator. Though the space-rocks were still striking the regolith behind them, they outran the immediate danger and settled into a steady if post-traumatic drive ...

Taji got up from his seat on the right side of the bus and moved over to the left side, sitting down next to Xing-Xing. They were both spacesuited, but neither suit nor circumstance could stop Taji from pursuing the object of what was by this time his extreme infatuation.

"I get it now," he said via intercom. "You wanted to go on a date with me the whole time, only you wanted to be the one to ask ME out."

Xing-Xing looked genuinely mystified.

"You like to be in charge," Taji continued. "I don't mind. Less work for ME."

"I truly don't know what you're talking about," Xing-Xing said.

"'Taji, get the goo-guns! Taji, follow me outside! Taji, grab hold of me! Taji, swing me around!' If that wasn't a date back there, I don't know what is. I've been to spin-the-bottle parties with less action!"

Even though they were racing away from certain death and in the direction of fathomless jeopardy, Xing-Xing broke out in a smile. Taji had charmed her. She leaned toward him until her helmet touched his. Then she pressed her lips to her helmet's super-strong plastic. Taji did the same—and they "kissed." Afterwards Taji whispered:

"Guess who felt tremors this time."

"Don't get used to it. That was only a thank-you for helping me with the goo-guns, not a promise of more to come."

In the rear of the vehicle, Byron and José Ignacio were shaking their heads at the rather disgusting "helmet-kissing" going on several seats ahead of them. They turned away from this wholly unnecessary spectacle to look out the glass of the bus at the silvery moonscape. It seemed they were moving in the general direction of Cosmopolis, as indicated by a cluster of abandoned vehicles in the distance: two mooncrawlers and a rockcrusher.

"How's the rescue-rocket gonna know where to find us now?" Byron said.

"I have a better question," José Ignacio replied. *"What are you planning on breathing until the rescue-rocket GETS here? It could be ten more hours. You've got about two hours left in your suit."*

Suddenly, and "out of the black" as the saying goes on the Moon, a rogue meteoroid slammed into the regolith mere yards ahead of them, causing the governor to swerve the bus hard to avoid crashing. But the vehicle lost traction in the process, then lost balance: it tipped over and tumbled into a small crater, triggering quite the surge of sound effects from its passengers (of the screaming variety).

Due to minimal gravity, the bus landed on its front grille with only minor impact, but now it was sitting vertically in the crater. The passengers were clustered around the driver's seat, on what was now the floor, except for Byron, who was clinging to the top of the bus, which had previously been the back seat. He jabbed at the handle on the rear door, managed to get it open, and called down to the others:

"This way's clear!"

Boy and robot climbed out onto what was now the roof of the vehicle, Byron calling back down:

"It's easy!"

But then, surveying the moonscape, Byron spotted trouble.

"More meteoroids are coming!" he shouted. *"I think they're gonna hit the bus!"*

Down by the driver's seat, Mrs. Barnett called back up:

"Jump out of the way! Byron, jump clear of the bus!"

From where they were semi-trapped, the Barnetts and Tangs saw Byron heed his mother's order and jump away. After that they lost sight of him, but right before the meteoroids struck they heard him confirm via intercom:

"I'm okay!"

A volley of space-rocks pounded the vehicle, knocking it deeper into the crater. Then another volley pummeled the area *around* the crater, sending boulders and moondust piling onto the glass bus until it was completely covered over—and dark as a dungeon inside.

A dim emergency light came on: Governor Tang had found the switch for it on the dashboard.

"Is anyone hurt?" he said.

They all shook their heads, all but Lucky, who was lying motionless, his eyes closed inside his helmet.

"Mr. von Stroganoff!" said Xing-Xing. She knocked on his helmet—which caused him to pop his eyes open.

"Sorry! Are we still here? I assumed we were done for!"

"We're alive," Taji confirmed. *"For a little longer anyway."*

Lucky looked around at the faintly lit portion of the over-turned bus in which they were now completely trapped. *"I'm not sure this was a bonus round worth winning,"* he grumbled.

"At least Byron got away," Mr. Barnett said.

"Got away where?" Lucky wanted to know. *"He's out on the surface of the Moon by himself!"*

"I'm beginning to think Byron could survive on the surface of the SUN by himself. Anyway, he has his robot with him. He has José Ignacio. They'll do all right."

Mrs. Barnett squeezed her husband's spacesuited hand for this statement of faith. But she wouldn't have time to express herself in words, because just now the bus was struck by the first in yet another volley of space-rocks. With each impact the vehicle shook more violently. The six remaining members of the group paired up, holding each other tight for comfort in this dire moment: Mr. Barnett holding Mrs. Barnett ... Taji holding Xing-Xing ... and Lucky clinging to Governor Tang—who was bearing it with gritted teeth.

"These blasted meteoroids aren't going to let up!" the governor shouted.

"We'll be pulverized!" Lucky moaned. *"I'm too handsome to die!"*

The impacts kept coming—gaining in volume and force.

"This is it!" Lucky said.

Taji gave Xing-Xing a goodbye squeeze. Mr. Barnett told his wife:

"Well, Mrs. Barnett, it's been grand! See you on the other side!"

And that's when the front "paw" of a rockcrusher burst through the top end of the bus. Next came the rockcrusher's enormous metal arm poking through the hole: it grabbed hold of the vehicle's steel rim and tore the bus open.

The freed passengers scrambled out and saw that the last round of meteoroids that had pounded their vehicle hadn't been meteoroids at all, it had been Byron! He was in the cockpit of the rockcrusher, which, to refresh memories, is a mining vehicle the shape of a grasshopper but the size of an elephant, skinned in titanium and fitted with an all-glass compartment to house its operator. Its operator, at the moment, was Byron, looking down at his parents, his brother, the Tangs, and Lucky, who were looking back up at him, thunderstruck.

Working the rockcrusher's joystick, Byron caused the vehicle to kneel so that the others could join him in the cockpit. Taji was first to climb in.

"Boon, you're two for two in the rescue department! Way to go!"

Byron's parents hugged him from both sides at the same time; and Lucky gave him a little bow of appreciation.

"That was brilliant!" Xing-Xing said.

"It truly was," chimed in Governor Tang. *"But tell me, Byron: how did you manage to work the controls?"*

"It's sorta self-explanatory," Byron said, using the joystick to demonstrate: *"Forward, backward, smashward."*

"Well, then," said the governor, *"since you've already mastered the vehicular arts, I propose we let you keep driving."*

This thrilled Byron, who back on Earth hadn't even been allowed to use a flight-pack yet, much less operate any type of motor vehicle on the ground, let alone something the size of a rockcrusher.

"Where to?" he asked the governor.

"Back to Cosmopolis. We need to find fresh oxygen-cartridges for our suits. Then we'll go park next to Crater Copernicus, to meet the rescue-rocket."

Byron settled back into the operator's seat, gripped the joystick, and started up the vehicle. Soon the rockcrusher was making great, grasshopper-like leaps across the lunar terrain. With seven people inside a cockpit built for two, it was quite cramped for the passengers, who kept banging into one another. But Byron himself was grinning with every leap, clicking his tongue in joy to the rockcrusher's rhythms ...

... until, horribly, the vehicle lurched to a halt. All the lights on the control panel started blinking—then went dark. Governor Tang flipped every switch on the dashboard—to no effect.

"What's WRONG with it?" Byron said, distressed not only that they were out of power to escape with, but that his driving time had been cut short.

"The battery's dead," explained the governor. *"The operator must've left the system running when the call came in to evacuate."*

"Must absolutely EVERYTHING keep going wrong?" Lucky wailed. *"I can't BEAR it! What do we do NOW?!"*

"We walk," said Governor Tang.

They climbed down out of the rockcrusher and tried to orient themselves in the lunar loneliness. Byron actually found the environment rather stimulating, with the blue orb of Earth looking so vivid in the distance—and it would be untrue to say he wasn't pleased at the idea of a hike across the Moon.

Xing-Xing detached a pair of mini-binoculars from her spacesuit and studied the way ahead; then she checked her spacesuit's oxometer.

"Bad news, everyone: I'd say it's two hours on foot to Cosmopolis and we only have an hour's oxygen left."

"We'll never make it!" Lucky cried out. *"We'll suffocate!"*

"We have no choice—we have to try," said the governor. *"It's our only option."*

"*Or maybe not,*" Byron mentioned.

Everyone swiveled to face him.

"*We're kinda close to where my class went on the field trip,*" he said, though for some reason that no one else understood yet, he didn't seem to want to admit it.

"*And?*" asked Mr. Barnett.

"*And the cave I found, I went into. It was too spelunkable NOT to.*"

"*And?!*" asked Mrs. Barnett, half-curious, half-furious.

Knowing he was confessing to many levels of bad behavior, but also worried that he wouldn't be believed, Byron's voice cracked into a little giggle in explaining:

"*And ... I sorta discovered an underground ecosystem there. With vegetation ... and a waterfall. And atmosphere.*"

A moment's silence followed.

"*That's impossible,*" said the governor.

"*I took off my helmet! I breathed air!*"

Everybody looked extremely dubious. Byron turned to José Ignacio for support—and for once the robot was ready to give it to him. "*Show them the leaf!*" he reminded Byron.

"*Oh, right!*" Byron unzipped his spacesuit's outer pocket and retrieved the green leaf he was storing there. "*Lookit! I plucked it off a plant in the cave!*"

The governor took possession of the leaf and held it up to his helmet to better examine it. "*This looks like a leaf of spinach from the Hydroponics Dome.*"

"*Well, it's not!*"

"*Boon,*" said Taji, "*you do understand that if we follow you to this cave and you're wrong about it, if the waterfall was some kind of weird rock formation and the plants were shadows from your flashlight, and you were only imagining it, then we won't have enough oxygen left to do anything but sit down and die.*"

"*But we already don't have enough oxygen to get anywhere else! And I didn't see rocks and shadows! I'm telling the truth!*"

"*I know you think you are, but are you sure this isn't like your biomass transducer that's really a vacuum cleaner or your lunar fort that's really a shack in the backyard or your seven-foot robot that's actually—*"

—Byron's eyes widened, so Taji stopped himself from saying "a twelve-inch toy," switching instead to another example:

"—*or the poster you had to have showing the Moon in crazy colors when we all know the Moon*—here he glanced around—*is really black and white?*"

"*I don't know about any of that,*" Byron said. "*But I repeat: I'm telling the truth.*"

Taji turned to his parents:

"*I believe him.*"

"*So do I,*" said Mrs. Barnett.

"*I do too,*" Mr. Barnett told the governor. "*Having an active imagination is one thing, but we didn't raise our son to be a liar.*"

Governor Tang remained skeptical, but he was a very bright man with excellent judgment: not for nothing had he been elected chief executive of the Moon three terms in a row. Calculating the relative danger of trying to reach Cosmopolis as opposed to trying to find oxygen elsewhere, he made his determination, double-checked his thinking, turned to look the youngest member of his band of refugees in the eye, and said:

"*Byron Barnett, lead on.*"

It was a moon montage: Byron led the group across the flats connecting two lunar ranges: mountains rising like Himalayas in sterling silver on either side of them. They were a single-file line of trekkers crossing the famously phrased "magnificent desolation" of the lunar surface.

Byron himself, at the front of the line, was feeling, fittingly, magnificent. He leapt onto a flat-topped rock and executed a "moonflip," capitalizing on the low gravity to somersault through the air and land without missing a step. Then he stopped, waiting for his fellow trekkers to follow his lead. Taji followed first: he executed a perfect moonflip of his own, almost twice as high as Byron's. Then Xing-Xing moonflipped, then Mr. and Mrs. Barnett. Even Governor Tang flipped nicely.

Finally it was Lucky's turn. Watching him make his approach to the flat-topped rock, José Ignacio began whispering to Byron, proposing new names for their easily nauseated traveling companion:

"*Barfy von Vomitoff? ... Queasy Upchuck-It-All? ... Retchy von Gag & Spew ... Pukey von Barf-A-Lot?*"

Lucky misstepped, tripped, and lost his grip on his case of diamonds. As he fell toward the regolith, the case hit the ground first and popped open, the diamonds inside all flying out and disappearing over the edge of a very small but unusually deep crater that the group had been skirting.

"*No!!!!!!!!!!!*" Lucky wailed, leaping after them. But a hand reached in to stop him: Governor Tang's. He grabbed Lucky by the leg to keep him from falling into the crater too, though Lucky kept clawing in vain for his gemstones.

Byron was watching all this with gloved hands over his bubble-helmet, peeking out between fingers. It took a whole minute for Lucky to stop howling about losing his diamonds, diamonds which, he insisted, were the only reason he'd stayed on the Moon in the first place rather than evacuating on the space-raft with everyone else. Once he'd resigned himself to this heinous twist of fate, he became a picture of gloom and moved to the back of the line to continue the trek in silence.

Soon the group was cresting the same ridge that Byron had found on this morning's field trip. Xing-Xing, checking her oxometer, told Taji:

"We have sixteen minutes of air left."

"He'll get us there," Taji said.

Byron began the descent down the ridge in great leaps. The others followed more cautiously, reaching the canyon floor without incident. From here it was a matter of following Byron to the cave entrance.

"There it is!" he called out, pointing to an opening in the rock wall. But then, looking disoriented, he swung around and said: *"Unless it's that cave on the other side."*

Following his sight line, everyone gasped in alarm at the great distance to the far side of the canyon.

"Just joking!" Byron said. *"This one's it!"*

He dashed into the cave. Their hearts all beating double-time from Byron's tease, the group followed without scolding him. They were too scared to put up a fight.

Inside the cave, they popped flashlights off spacesuits and began walking. Xing-Xing again checked the dial on her oxometer and in another aside to Taji whispered:

"Four minutes of air."

Even Taji was nervous by now that his brother might not get them to their destination in time. His concern only grew when the group reached the cave's inner abyss, and Byron said:

"This way!"

He jumped straight down the hole.

Not liking it, the others jumped in after him, floating and twirling their way down.

Lucky retched in descent. He nearly vomited, but to his credit he managed to swallow the uprushing puke before he touched down.

Once the group was reassembled at the bottom of the abyss, they followed Byron through a long tunnel of rock, until, at last, via flashlight, they spotted up ahead the thick curtain of leaf-bearing vines that Byron had discovered earlier in the day.

"I don't believe it!" said Governor Tang. He touched the vegetation, crunching it between gloved fingers. *"They're actual vines. Dried up and dead, but real."*

"They're not dead on the other side," Byron promised. He pushed through the thick green curtain, the group tagging along closely…

On the other side, they emerged into a sub-lunar chamber that none of them could've imagined. Though still visible only by dint of flashlights, it was just the way Byron had described it: an underground world of blue-green fauna with a small waterfall running through the middle.

Governor Tang confirmed that the curtain of vines was indeed alive on this side. Shaking his head in equal parts wonder and confusion, he pulled back the vines in a large swath, revealing a heavy, green plastic drape between the inner and outer layers of vegetation. *"Auto-sealant!"* he shouted. *"This place didn't grow, it was BUILT!"*

At this very moment a bank of artificial lights snapped on, bathing the chamber in warm, sun-like radiation and revealing the scope of this miraculous ecosystem. Among the lush vegetation were beautifully flowering plants which immediately drew Mrs. Barnett's eye. But what interested Xing-Xing was the chamber's control panel. She stepped over to investigate, calling back to the others:

"The lights are on a timer. I'll change the setting so they won't go off."

Byron unlatched and removed his helmet. He took in a big gulp of air, exhaling slowly. Governor Tang followed suit. Then everyone else did too.

Checking her oxometer, Xing-Xing said:

"Twenty-six seconds to spare."

The Brothers Barnett eyed each other. "You're three for three!" Taji signaled, using only his fingers to communicate. On a day of many satisfactions, this put the biggest grin of all on Byron's face.

CHAPTER: 11

"WHERE ARE WE?" wondered Mr. Barnett out loud while marveling at the range of vegetation in this sub-lunar ecosystem that Byron had led them to. Not only were there trees and ferns, but a wildly overgrown vegetable garden of carrots, spinach, cauliflower, Brussels sprouts, bok choy, purple potatoes, and baby pumpkins (though pumpkins are actually a fruit). And beneath the waterfall grew a lush patch of orange seaweed, lately confirmed by science to be a kind of superfood.

"Come look at this!" called Governor Tang from around a corner. Everyone scurried to catch up to him. They found him standing in front of a cave within the cave, its innards all sparkly from reflected light.

"Lucky, I believe you can tell us what we're looking at."

"It's a diamond mine," Lucky whispered in awe, "formed in an ancient lava tube."

"As in a lava tube to a volcano?" Taji said. "The Moon has volcanoes?"

"It *used* to have them," explained Xing-Xing, the one true Lunarian in the group and even better than her father at lunar history. "Three and a half billion years ago, this was all eruptions and molten rock."

"Byron," said Governor Tang, "I believe you've discovered the underground palace of J. Marcus Mingus. This is the secret abode of Moonbeard Marc. And the legendary source of his wealth." Watching Lucky run his hand along the thousands of rough diamonds embedded in the rock of this ancient lava tube, the governor added:

"There's no private land on the Moon, so under normal circumstances, diamonds belong to whoever finds them. In this case, however, I should tell you that I'm going to designate this entire cave and all its contents an Historic Lunar Landmark, meaning it'll become a trust of the Lunar League and preserved just as it is. But before I do that, Lucky, why don't you take a few stones. To replace the ones you lost."

"I *suppose* I could," Lucky said unenthusiastically.

Lucky's lack of appreciation for the governor's gesture spurred Mrs. Barnett to give him a small scolding:

"It's not every day a person receives an offer of free diamonds, Lucky. You don't seem very excited about it."

"No, no, it's lovely that I'll have replacement gems, but correct me if I'm wrong, Mrs. Barnett: won't I still be trapped right here with them? It took half a century and a boy-explorer with the energy of a stellar explosion to find this cave. We have no portable oxygen to leave it again, and the rescue-rocket has no way of finding us or even knowing we're down here."

"True," Mrs. Barnett said.

"Let's keep looking around," suggested Xing-Xing. "Maybe there's an old radio we can use to send a signal."

This being an excellent proposal, as so many of Xing-Xing's proposals were, the group dispersed into various chambers of the extensive cave to see what they could find. Xing-Xing and Taji were the first to make a major discovery: a machine room full of whirring equipment, pumps, clusters of wires and bunches of bound copper tubes.

"Here's the atomic generator that's been keeping the power on," confirmed Xing-Xing, " ... and here's the recycling mechanism for the artificial waterfall ... and the irrigation lines for the vegetation ... and the air filtration pumps. It's clunky stuff, very old-school, but it works."

"Think of the diamonds it cost him to build all this," said Taji, "and the hush-money he must've paid out to keep this place a secret!"

Nearby, Mr. and Mrs. Barnett had found and were now exploring the cave's rather modest living quarters. Next to the living quarters, Governor Tang and Lucky had found a fifty-foot-tall chamber housing a telescope as big as the really big telescopes in the best observatories on Earth. The scope's lens was peeking through the rock at the top of this portion of the cave, sealed with a rubber lid to keep the air in.

Byron too had made a discovery: another high-ceilinged room containing a small rocket-ship sitting upright on its launch pad. Directly above it and fitted into the top of the cave was a steel iris which presumably opened up when the rocket lifted off, providing an outlet for the ship to shoot through. The body of the rocket was only eight feet tall. Byron circled it slowly, until he came to the front portion, made of tempered glass—whereupon his eyes almost burst from their sockets.

"Everybody!!!" he hollered.

"Did you find something?!" called his mother from some adjacent chamber.

"Yes!!!"

"What is it?!"

"Ummm ... Moonbeard Marc!!!"

The group came sprinting in and found Byron beside the little glass-paneled rocket-ship. Inside it Moonbeard Marc was positioned upright as if in a casket, wearing his oldtimer's spacesuit, his gloves and helmet beside him. His body was shrunken a bit but otherwise intact, including the dozens of diamonds braided into his long beard and hair.

"It's a space-coffin!" Byron said.

"What's he holding?" asked Taji.

Moonbeard Marc's hand lay on a small metal object. Mr. Barnett put on his eyeglasses and peered through the rocket's glass casing. "That's a triggering device. Old Mr. Mingus probably climbed in when he knew he was about to expire and positioned his hand to fall on it when he gave up the ghost. Looks like the connection failed." Mr. Barnett took his glasses off again, absentmindedly setting them down on a rock shelf beside the space-coffin.

"But why isn't he a skeleton by now?" asked Byron.

"Because he's in a vacuum," Mr. Barnett said. "The air was pumped out when he powered up. His skin dried, but there weren't any microbes to break down the flesh."

"So he's a mummy! Maybe we can see through his nostrils straight into his brain!" Clicking on his flashlight, Byron jumped up onto the rock shelf to get himself high enough to look into Moonbeard Marc's nostrils—and stepped directly onto his father's eyeglasses.

"Byron!"

"Sorry!!!"

"Oh, Byron, this is not *good*."

Byron bit his lip. Then asked nervously:

"Don't you have your spares?"

"In my blazer. On my dresser. In my bedroom. At Cosmopolis."

Grasping the seriousness of his blunder, Byron threw himself into such a monumental apology that his father had no choice but to forgive him. Xing-Xing, meanwhile, went over to examine the launch-chamber's wall of machinery.

"Is there a radio?" Governor Tang asked her.

"No. This man was a true hermit. But I see why his capsule didn't blast off: there was a short in the sequencing system: it's all blown out."

Governor Tang whirled to face Mr. Barnett. "If we could patch it up," he said, "why couldn't we send up the capsule as a kind of flare when the rescue-rocket passes overhead? They'd see the fire-trail and be able to follow it straight down to us."

"But how will we know when the rescue-rocket's overhead?" Taji said.

"There's a telescope in the next chamber. I'll stay glued to the eyepiece." To Mr. Barnett the governor added: "Barnett, you're the best engineer Amalgamated MegaPhysics ever produced. Surely you can fix a fifty-year-old sequencing system."

"I'm afraid not, Mr. Governor. I have hyperopia. I'm far-sighted. Things in the distance I have no trouble with, but up close, without my glasses, I'm blind as a bat without sonar."

Disappointment all around was the result of this admission, while Lucky, in his mind at least, started to actually panic. But then Mr. Barnett finished his thought, telling the governor: "However, as I've tried explaining every time it comes up, I'm only the *second* best engineer AmPhys ever produced."

"That information would matter more to me," said the governor grimly, "if you could snap your fingers and deliver me the top man."

"Who says I can't?"

It took a moment for the governor to understand; then, when he did, he turned to Mrs. Barnett.

"I give you the former Bianca Barcelona," announced Mr. Barnett proudly. "The best engineer there ever was."

"Until I got a better job offer as CEO of the Barnett Family," Mrs. Barnett said. "The hours were worse, but I liked the perks."

"Well, *well!*" said the governor. "You Barnetts are one talented clan! To Mrs. Barnett he added: "Now, Barnett, let's find you a toolkit and get you started!"

Within the hour, Mrs. Barnett had opened up the wall of machinery in the launch-chamber and was deep into the task of repairing the space-capsule's sequencing system, with Xing-Xing and Taji assigned to help out by handing her the tools she needed one tool at a time. Mrs. Barnett's job was a large one, akin to taking apart a hovercraft engine to locate a worn-out part the size of a hairpin before replacing it and putting the engine back together again. Dozens of pieces of the dismantled sequencing system were now laid out neatly on a shelf, waiting for the hairpin to be found.

Mrs. Barnett herself, wearing safety goggles, was wedged inside the bank of machinery, beyond sight of Xing-Xing and Taji. Xing-Xing stood between the machinery and Taji; Taji stood at a workbench where he'd laid out all the tools from the toolkit.

"Wire strippers!" said Mrs. Barnett from inside the wall.

"Wire strippers!" Xing-Xing repeated to Taji at the workbench.

"Wire strippers!" confirmed Taji, selecting the requested tool. He winked at Xing-Xing with his right eye as he passed it over.

"Um, these would be bolt cutters," said Xing-Xing, "*those* are the wire strippers."

Unembarrassed, Taji selected the correct tool and passed it along. "Wire strippers!" he said again, winking at Xing-Xing with his left eye this time.

Half-flirting back at him, Xing-Xing said:

"Don't be winking at me! This is a life-or-death operation! You need to concentrate!"

"Winking *helps* me concentrate."

"Mole grips!" called Mrs. Barnett from inside the wall.

"Mole grips!" repeated Xing-Xing.

Taji turned back to the workbench, but hesitated selecting a tool. Xing-Xing could hardly believe the things this Earth-boy didn't know. "Second from the left," she said, shaking her head.

"Mole grips!" confirmed Taji, passing them along.

"Are you really the son of two brilliant engineers?" Xing-Xing teased. But Taji was a master of turning a tease his own way. "I know!" he said. "Thank goodness being an egghead can *skip* a generation!"

"That's not what I meant."

Taji only smiled. And unlike his little brother's various facial expressions, Taji's smile usually *did* do the trick. "So in the end," he told Xing-Xing, "I guess you'd have to say this whole day has turned into one long date."

"In a very strange way."

"So if we don't manage to signal the rescue-rocket and this really *is* doomsville down here, and I turn out to be the last boy you ever kissed, would you say you went out in style?"

"I'd say it's a flawed hypothetical."

"Why's that?"

"Because I have confidence your mother's going to get us off the Moon."

"So ... what you're saying is, you want to start dating me back on Earth."

Xing-Xing was sure by now that never in her life had she met a boy with more chutzpah than Taji; but before she could say so:

"Monkey wrench!" Mrs. Barnett called out.

"Monkey wrench!" Xing-Xing repeated.

"Monkey wrench!" Taji confirmed.

In the cave's lava tube, Lucky was using a chisel and hammer to dislodge diamonds from the rock wall, his jacket pocket bulging with ones he'd already collected. At the moment he was working on freeing up a very large and no doubt extremely valuable stone.

"Don't take more than you lost," warned Byron, watching from the mouth of the tube.

"What are you, the Moon Police? I heard what the governor said!" With a good thump on his chisel Lucky loosened the diamond and yanked it out. "There! I'm done!"

He exited the tube in a rare state of satisfaction and sat down with Byron at a small picnic-type table in the adjacent chamber. There his mood turned morose again. Examining his new gems, he complained:

"I don't know why I bothered: there's no guarantee we're ever getting *out* of this sub-lunar prison."

"Will you whack a diamond for me?" Byron said.

"I don't think so."

"Oh, come on!"

"You know my sad history with diamond-cutting! It's what sent me up here in the first place!"

"But what else do we have to do? Please? I want to see you whack it!"

"It's exceptionally delicate work, Byron. If I'm off even by a hair's breadth, I'll shatter the stone."

"You're gonna have to start again sooner or later. Might as well be now, where it's only me watching. I won't be mean if you mess up."

Lucky thought it over, sighed in his sing-songy way, removed his loupe from a pocket and fitted it into his eye like a monocle. Next he placed the chisel against the largest of the new stones, raised the hammer, got ready to whack it, and:

"Good luck!" Byron cheered.

Lucky brought the hammer down right onto the table, missing the stone entirely.

"Byron!"

"Sorry! I didn't want you to be nervous!"

"I *wasn't* nervous! But I am *now!*"

"Take a deep breath and try again."

While Lucky shook off his agitation, Byron turned to José Ignacio and made an exaggerated face—including an out-stuck tongue—apropos Lucky's chance of success. But Lucky surprised him: he raised his hammer a second time and brought it down hard against the chisel. The stone split neatly in half, revealing a smooth interior facet of the diamond. It was, indeed, a masterful whack.

"Nice job!" Byron said. "Keep going!"

In the observatory-chamber, Governor Tang was looking through the eyepiece to the telescope. He saw the rescue-rocket on the far side of a vast, rotating cluster of meteoroids: the ship was apparently waiting for the space-rocks to clear before making the crossing to the Moon.

Next he turned a knob on the fifty-foot scope, zooming in on the white worm itself, which had drifted by this time to the near side of Mars. It was the back half of the worm to be precise, two and a half thousand miles long, with an electrical coil around the rear that packed enough voltage to have zapped open and tunneled through the very stuff of space.

Something about it alarmed him. Fiddling with the scope's controls, he increased the magnification and looked back through the eyepiece. Now he could see the worm up-close. Something odd was definitely happening to it: something huge inside of it was trying to squeeze through and pop out, something too big for it, a round object causing it to balloon up in the middle, the way a swallowed ostrich egg would balloon the body of a snake.

Again the governor worked the scope's control for greater magnification—until he reached its maximum setting. Again he looked through the eyepiece, still trying to see into the worm, still trying to get an angle on the danger, still trying to figure out what was coming next. It took a good twenty minutes, during which he had to try to blink as little as possible. Then, finally, he saw it: the round object making slow but definite progress through the body of the worm had just begun to peek out of the worm's anal situation. Recognizing it for what it was, the governor gulped in dread. Because what was inside the white worm trying to come out was nothing less than some other solar system's full-sized moon.

In the cave's main chamber, prevented from being much help to anybody else due to the accidental crushing of his eyeglasses by Byron, Mr. Barnett was instead taking care of a piece of personal business. He was collecting a bouquet of assorted flowers from the artificial ecosystem's various forms of plant life. True, some of the flowers were more the sprigs from vegetables than actual blossoms, but when trapped in the closed system of a sub-lunar cave, it pays to use your imagination.

Eventually Mr. Barnett decided to check out some of the other chambers for further floral possibilities, which is when he came across Lucky and Byron near the lava tube.

"Dad, come over here! Look what Lucky did!"

Lucky had by now whacked away at his diamond in the rough, gaining confidence as he went along, slicing the stone into a beautiful, multifaceted jewel. Mr. Barnett stepped up at just the right moment to see Lucky whack it one last time.

"That's fine work, Lucky. I'd like to buy it from you."

Lucky made a strange face, the kind of face you make when you hear a joke you don't think is as funny as the joke-teller thinks it is.

"I'm in the market for a diamond for Mrs. Barnett," Mr. Barnett said. "This is just what I had in mind."

"Yes, well, the real question is, who *doesn't* dream of owning a von Stroganoff diamond?"

"How much?"

"I'm awfully sorry, Mr. Barnett, but if you have to ask, you can't afford to buy."

"Oh, don't be a snob. I'll give you half a pack of gum for it."

Mr. Barnett pulled the half a pack in question out of his jacket pocket and slapped it on the table. He would've offered the whole pack, but he'd chewed a few pieces on the way up from Earth aboard *The Biarritz*. So half a pack was his best and final offer.

"You cannot be serious," Lucky sniffed.

"Think of it this way: if we're stuck here, the gum's worth more than the gem. If we're rescued, you can always chip off one more stone to take home with you."

Lucky made a cross-eyed face, groaned his botheration, and said:

"First I'll need to taste-test."

"Naturally."

Lucky popped a piece of gum in his mouth and chewed in irritation for several seconds. The flavor, spicy orange, was actually one of his favorites. Still, he didn't seem to want to make the trade. Turning to Byron for support, he said:

"Purely on principle, swapping a Stroganoff for only half a pack of gum feels deeply unjust."

"Such is life," Byron replied with a shrug of his shoulders.

Lucky pouted about it for another few seconds, then gave in. "Fine," he said, complaining even while agreeing.

Mr. Barnett reached for the diamond on the table, but Lucky smacked him away. "You can't just press a gemstone into a lady's hand all on its own! Not even a Stroganoff!"

"Why not?" asked Byron.

"It's not a marble! What's she supposed to do, carry it around in her pocket?"

"What's wrong with *that*?"

Lucky rolled his eyes at Byron and turned back to Mr. Barnett. "Come along, then. Let's find you a suitable setting."

In the launch-chamber, Mrs. Barnett finished sealing a bundle of wires inside the bank of machinery that she'd been working on, then stepped out and told Xing-Xing and Taji:

"Let's close her up."

"Ladies," said Taji, "I think I can handle this."

With Mrs. Barnett and Xing-Xing exchanging amused glances, Taji put some muscle into the proposition, pushing the bank of machinery back into place. Afterwards he was clearly pleased with himself, which only made Xing-Xing shake her head at him one more time.

"Now we fire up the sequencer," said Mrs. Barnett. She flipped a switch. "We'll just let the tubes warm up and see if the system takes the current."

This is when Mr. Barnett entered the chamber, one hand behind his back. "Mrs. Barnett," he said, "could I see you over here by the space-coffin?"

Mrs. Barnett crossed the chamber to join him, leaving Taji and Xing-Xing to watch them from a distance. Lucky and Byron were here too, looking in from the archway into the hall.

With a warm little laugh, Mrs. Barnett whispered to her husband:

"A mysterious rendezvous beside a space-coffin with a dashing, farsighted man. Intriguing."

"I have something for you."

"Even better. Go on."

From behind his back Mr. Barnett pulled out a bouquet of handpicked flowers and ferns. "Roses," he said. "More or less." From his jacket pocket he produced the gem bought from Lucky, set into a pendant necklace made out of vines. "And diamonds."

"Well, dia*mond*," said Mrs. Barnett.

"Be that as it may, let the record show, whether we leave here or we remain, that before my work was done, I kept my word to the goddess who married me. Roses and diamonds are what I promised her for agreeing to become my wife, and roses and diamonds, give or take, are what I've delivered."

"Wallace, they're beautiful." She kissed him, which even Byron found acceptable to watch this one time, though normally such public displays of affection were, of course, revolting.

"And this diamond is ex*qui*site!" Mrs. Barnett said, examining the stone in its attractive if vegetative pendant. "Though I don't know how you could possibly afford it!"

"Ah, well, what's money to a man in love?"

Across the chamber, the wall of machinery suddenly lit up and began beeping. Mrs. Barnett left her husband by the space-coffin to confirm the status of her repairs just as Governor Tang appeared through the archway.

"Good news, Mr. Governor!" called Mrs. Barnett. "The sequencing system is fixed: this bird will fly!"

"I'm afraid my news is less pleasant: the white worm is drifting closer, it's halfway between us and Mars—and next time it's not going to shoot out any mere meteoroids, it's about to eject a full-sized moon that it swallowed on the other end and that's been struggling to squeeze through."

"A whole *moon's* stuck in it?" Byron said.

"A whole moon. And when it finally *does* shoot out, unless I've guessed wrong, it's going to smash into *our* moon and blast us into a hundred trillion pieces."

Xing-Xing was first to realize the consequences:

"But daddy, without the Moon, Earth might deviate from its orbit. That could mean scorching heat in the Arctic and freezing cold in the tropics. Ecologically it would be the end of the world."

"The end of the *world*?" cried Lucky. "What about the end of *us*?!"

"That too," said Xing-Xing, causing Lucky to gag, heave, and throw up his lunch of butternut squash soup, cheese soufflé, and Parker House rolls, right there on the floor of the cave.

For once his vomit seemed exactly the right reaction.

CHAPTER: 12

"HOW WOULD ONE STOP a white worm if one had a mind to?" asked Governor Tang. He and the group were still in the launch-chamber of Moonbeard Marc's cave, mulling over what the governor had discovered by telescope and reported to his fellow refugees, that the white worm was about to expel a full-sized moon of its own. This other moon's trajectory would bring it right at them, shattering *their* moon: *Earth's* moon. As a result, Earth itself might deviate from its orbit. This would trigger violent changes in weather around the globe, disrupting ecosystems worldwide, killing millions of creatures and putting the human race itself at risk of extinction.

Replying to the governor's question about how to stop a white worm, Mr. Barnett mused:

"Well, its neutronic composition *is* fundamentally unstable."

Mrs. Barnett gasped and her face lit up: she knew just what Mr. Barnett was thinking. "The overcharged quarks at its core are just this side of super-saturation!" she said.

"Exactly!" Mr. Barnett confirmed, the two of them going giddy with their idea, whatever it was.

"So in theory," Mrs. Barnett said, "any sufficient energy injection could trigger the effect."

"Trigger *what* effect?" Governor Tang wanted to know.

"The crystallization effect," Mrs. Barnett said.

"In which the white worm's carbon atoms all bond together into a tetrahedral lattice," added Mr. Barnett.

"Tetrahedral lattice, tetrahedral lattice," Byron said to himself in a low voice. "Where have I heard about a tetrahedral lattice before?"

"Um, in the lodge at Crater Copernicus?" José Ignacio noted. "When I explained to you that that's all a diamond is? Carbon atoms bonded together in a tetrahedral lattice? Remember?"

"A space diamond!" Byron shouted. "If you trigger a super-saturation effect inside the white worm's quarky core, it'll turn into a diamond! A diamond *worm*!"

Byron's parents both whirled to face him.

"That's exactly right," said Mrs. Barnett, deeply impressed and, to be quite candid, more than a little surprised that Byron had grasped it.

"Sorry," said the governor. "Are you telling me that if you inject enough energy into the worm, you'll turn it into a giant diamond?"

"That's what physics predicts," said Mr. Barnett. "Theoretically."

"The process should freeze it in place," Mrs. Barnett clarified. "And shut it down."

"But where would that kind of energy come from?" asked Xing-Xing.

"Well," said Mrs. Barnett, "in principle, any garden-variety atomic blast could do the job. If we took Moonbeard Marc out of his capsule, we could install the cave's atomic generator in his place and rig it to explode by remote."

"In the interest of full disclosure," Mr. Barnett disclosed fully, "I should point out that if we shoot the atomic generator into space, we'd only have what power was left down here in the system batteries. Once that ran out, we'd be in the dark."

"Ex*cuse* me!" Lucky interjected. "If we use the capsule to shoot at this worm, how are we going to use the capsule as a flare to signal the rescue-rocket?!"

"We might not be able to do both," admitted Governor Tang.

"Then I say we signal the rocket and get ourselves rescued *first*. Once we're back on Earth, *then* we can worry about the white worm."

"If we don't shut this worm down quickly," the governor countered, "there won't be a Moon for us to be rescued *from*, let alone much of an Earth worth going back *to*."

"And if we *do* shut this worm down," argued Lucky, "we'll never be heard from again! We'll end up a bunch of mummies in a cave, just like Moonbeard Marc!"

"We may have to make that sacrifice, yes."

"Or," suggested Xing-Xing, "we could try to wait until the rescue-rocket is exactly overhead before we fire the capsule. We'd be shooting the white worm and signaling for help at the same time. After all, we don't know how long we have before the worm expels *its* moon. We might have enough time."

"I don't like the odds," grumbled Lucky.

"Let's vote on it!" Byron chimed in. "Who votes to save the human race?" he said, raising his own hand. Everyone else did likewise—except for Lucky. "Who votes for the end of the world?" Byron continued. He and everyone else put their hands down. They all stared at Lucky, waiting to see how he would vote.

"I rather think you've turned this into a trick question," he muttered.

Byron kept quiet—mostly because he didn't know what to say. Then Lucky gave in:

"Fine. Save the human race." He grunted in total exasperation but raised his hand anyway, making the decision unanimous. Byron was delighted to be able to declare the results of his little election:

"Let's go bomb a worm!!!"

Forty minutes later, Admiral Haddad's rescue-rocket had reached lunar orbit. On the ship's bridge, the admiral herself was leading the search for the stranded colonists, using a hyper-scope to scan the surface of the Moon below. Deputy Olafsson, seated beside her, was looking through a hyper-scope of his own. When Crater Copernicus came into view, admiral and deputy gasped in unison.

"It's gone!" said Deputy Olaffson. "The lodge is *gone!*"

Admiral Haddad ordered her navigator to take the ship down so they could hover over the crater. Soon they were close enough to see what had happened: the old lodge had toppled to the crater floor and been destroyed by fire from the inside out.

"They couldn't have survived that," said the admiral.

"Unless they managed to get out before it happened," Deputy Olafsson said.

A short debate followed over what to do next. The floor of Crater Copernicus was too lumpy for this enormous flagship of the Astral Corps to land on safely. Instead they would have to find a flatter spot up above and send a team down into the crater by foot to explore the debris of the lodge for the bodies of the colonists. In this way they could confirm what had happened to Governor Tang and his group, then bring their remains back to Earth for a proper burial.

But if the colonists *had* escaped the lodge before it was destroyed, they might be wandering the lunar surface at this very moment, short on oxygen and in need of immediate rescue. The time it would take to explore the lodge could be too long for them to wait. So even though the governor and his group might already be dead, it made sense to take a leap of faith and first go looking to see if they were alive, rather than the other way around.

"We'll overfly a radius of twenty miles from the crater," ordered the admiral. "Just to be sure."

Mrs. Barnett entered the observatory-chamber carrying a trigger-box that she'd improvised from spare parts in the cave's machine room. Xing-Xing and Taji came in next, Xing-Xing unspooling wire on a spindle that was connected both to the trigger-box that Mrs. Barnett was carrying and to Moonbeard Marc's space-capsule in its launch-chamber several rooms over. Taji's job was to make sure the wire didn't snag on anything along the way.

Already in the observatory-chamber were: Governor Tang, keeping his eye on the telescope's eyepiece; Mr. Barnett, standing beside him to keep him company; Lucky, pacing in circles; and on the far side of the chamber, Byron and José Ignacio, seated in a rocky niche.

"I see the rescue-rocket on the horizon!" the governor called out.

"Fire right now!" Lucky shouted. "Fire right now and they'll spot us!"

"Settle down, Lucky!" scolded Mrs. Barnett. "I have to arm the trigger first. We'll wait for the rocket to make another pass." She began working on the trigger-box, to arm it, but the governor, who'd just swiveled the telescope for a different view, suddenly advised:

"The worm's about to blow its moon! We have to blast it as quick as we can—there may not be time to wait for the rescue-rocket to circle back!"

With a terrible tension bearing down on the adults, Byron, across the room in his niche, was looking unusually calm.

"Why are you so quiet?" José Ignacio whispered. "It's disturbing me."

"Ssshh! I'm conducting a thought experiment."

"I don't like the sound of that."

"*Aha!*"

"Oh, no."

"José Ignacio, we have to get out of here!"

"Don't be a madman! This is no time for exploring!"

"This isn't about exploring, it's about *existing*!"

"Oh, for goodness' sake. Must you always be so Byronic?"

"Excuse me? What does 'Byronic' mean?"

"It's, you know, how you are."

"How *am* I?"

"You know—*Byronic*. I don't know how else to say it. You do things Byronically, in a way normal people would never think of. Byronic!"

But Byron simply didn't have the time to discuss it any further—he was already on his feet and yanking at both José Ignacio's claws.

"Get up, get up, get *up*!"

Despite himself, the robot allowed Byron to pull him out of their niche. With the memory bulb in his transparent cranium flaring frantically, he followed Byron through a tunnel of rock into Moonbeard Marc's quarters. Here Byron began yanking open drawers and overturning bins, rummaging for some very particular item.

"What are you *looking* for?" demanded José Ignacio.

"Found 'em!" Byron said from the inside of a walk-in locker.

"Found *what*? What's *in* there?"

Byron emerged from the locker with a bundle of skyrockets in hand.

"Fireworks?" asked José Ignacio. "You were looking for fireworks?"

"After he disappeared, Moonbeard Marc used to send 'em up every year on his birthday. The reason nobody else could ever figure out where he was sending 'em up *from* is cause they were always watching from somewhere on the surface, like back at Cosmopolis, where they didn't have a big-picture view. But if they'd been in a rocket-ship gliding *over* the Moon, they would've seen the fireworks right away and been able to follow the fire-trail straight down, right to right here!"

"Why doesn't that sound completely insane to me?"

"José Ignacio, we gotta get to the surface and shoot these off when the rescue-rocket comes back, so they can find us! If my mom has to fire at the white worm before the rescue-rocket's in sight, these fireworks'll be our one chance to signal for help!"

"But what about oxygen? If we go up to the surface, what are you going to *breathe*?"

"I can answer that!"

He darted into the sleeping chamber. On its bed Governor Tang had laid out the mummified body of J. Marcus Mingus, aka Moonbeard Marc. As per the plan, the body had been removed from its space-coffin to make room for the atomic generator, turning the coffin into a missile with nuclear kick.

José Ignacio followed Byron into the sleeping chamber just in time to see Byron fingering the mummy exploratorily. "What are you *doing* to him?" the robot said. "You can't go poking around a dead person!"

"I just need to check his oxometer!" He found the dial he was looking for on the spacesuit's elbow, read it, and called out: "It still has air! Help me get it off him!"

"Get *what* off him?"

"His spacesuit! I'm gonna wear it up to the surface!"

With José Ignacio voicing his disapproval, he and Byron extracted the diamond-bearded corpse from its spacesuit. Byron then slipped on the suit over his clothes, gathered the crucial fireworks in a bag, and raced for the cave's exit, José Ignacio flying beside him. They leapt through the vine-covered auto-sealant and into the long tunnel of rock; but here, in low gravity again, Byron found it difficult walking, let alone running. The problem was Moonbeard Marc's spacesuit—made for a man over six feet tall and now being worn by a boy only a few inches over four feet. Flopping along in the oversized suit, Byron finally tripped on his own boot and fell.

"*That spacesuit's too big for you!*" José Ignacio complained pointlessly.

"*I know that!*" Byron shot back. "*Stop obnoxicating and help me up!*"

"*There's no such word as 'obnoxicating.'* "

"*Um, yes, there most certainly is. 'Obnoxicating?' Like 'intoxicating?'* "

They were speaking via intercom again now that they were in the airless void of the Moon, even down here in the sub-lunar sector. Giving in to Byron, José Ignacio extended a claw to help him up, after which they scurried into the vertical portion of the cave, pulling themselves up toward the surface.

Back in the observatory-chamber, no one had noticed that Byron was gone: they were too engrossed in their urgent work to launch the space-coffin-slash-atomic-missile.

"Hurry!" Governor Tang called out, his eye to the telescope. "The rescue-rocket's circling back!"

"The button's stuck!" said Mrs. Barnett, fiddling with the trigger-box.

"This is giving me an ulcer!" Lucky moaned.

"Too late!" the governor said. "The rocket's over the horizon! Oh, *no*!"

"What is it?" said Mr. Barnett. The governor stepped aside so Mr. Barnett could look through the eyepiece.

"Pops, what do you see?" Taji said.

"The worm's about to eject its moon! Fire the capsule! We can't wait for the rescue-rocket to come back! We have to fire right *now*!"

Mrs. Barnett dug into the side of the stuck button on the trigger-box using the polished nail of her index finger, cracking her nail for the cause. "Got it!" she said, loosening the button and pressing it hard.

Moonbeard Marc's underground palace rumbled from end to end as the space-coffin in its launch-chamber blasted off. The steel iris above it dilated to make an egress from the cave; then, after the rocket was up and away, the iris closed shut again.

Up on the surface, Byron and José Ignacio stopped setting up their fireworks long enough to watch the capsule roar out of the ground and rise into space. The white worm it was heading toward was now visible to the naked eye if you knew which part of the lunar sky to look for it in, which Byron did. As a consequence of being stretched and swollen by the huge moon it was about to expel, the worm had reached the point of maximum menace to everything—and every*one*—in its path.

When the capsule bearing its atomic payload shrank to a shiny dot racing into space, Byron turned his attention back to the business at hand: the fireworks. *"Let's do a test before the rescue-rocket comes back,"* he told José Ignacio. *"Just to be safe."* He took a long-stemmed lighter from the bag he was carrying and pulled its trigger, producing a small flame.

"How can that work without oxygen?" asked the robot. *"Fire needs air to feed it."*

"There's an oxygen tube on the inside."

"Ah. Clever."

Byron touched the flame to the fuse of a skyrocket: it took off wildly, zigzagging over the regolith before slamming into a canyon wall.

"Not the result one was hoping for," said José Ignacio.

At the same time, back in the cave's observatory-chamber, the rest of the group was about to have better luck with their own operation-in-progress.

"The capsule's almost at the worm!" said Governor Tang, following their homemade missile through Moonbeard Marc's immense telescope.

Mrs. Barnett readied her finger on the detonator.

"Now!" called the governor.

Mrs. Barnett pressed the blinking button on the detonator, sending an infrared wave vital to the survival of the human race up through the ceiling of the cave, up over the surface of the Moon, up through the mileage of space, past the Earth, almost to Mars, right up to the infrared receptor node that she'd installed on the side of what had until today been Moonbeard Marc's unlaunched space-coffin.

Everyone in the cave held their breath—and Lucky even cut into his bottom lip with his front tooth—because there was a length of time equal to several heartbeats in which they did not know whether their plan would succeed or fail. But Mrs. Barnett was no less than the brilliant engineer that Mr.

Barnett had claimed. Her atomic enema injected itself into the white worm's rectum exactly as intended ... and blew up! ... sending a storm of energy straight through to the worm's quarky, nearly super-saturated core.

The worm wriggled, twisted, shivered, and shook.

Next came a long and excruciating moment—in which nothing happened. For a hundred miles around the white worm everything went still, like a lake after the ripples from a skipping stone have settled.

But only because there's no sound in the vacuum of space could you not tell that something was happening deep *inside* the worm's worminess. If there *had* been sound in space, you would've known that something big was going on, because it would've sounded like a hundred thousand garbage trucks grinding a million empty bottles.

Then, all at once, you could *see* what was happening: from the inside out, the white worm was freezing up into a tetrahedral lattice, transforming from raw energy into pure diamond. By the time it was done, it was, in point of scientific fact, the biggest diamond in the universe, a giant jewel hanging there in outer space.

However: in the split-instant before the worm crystallized and the transformation was complete, it happened to shrink a few hundred meters in the process. Why mention this? Because *as* it shrank, it crunched down hard on the half-exposed moon that had been on the point of shooting out, breaking it into a centillion bits, which is a number many times larger than a trillion, a number, to be specific, written as the number "one thousand" followed by three hundred zeros, a number to boggle the brain. So numerous and therefore so small were the centillion bits of this moon from the other side of the universe that they posed no further threat to the Earth or its neighbors. They simply scattered to the edges of the solar system: harmless space-rubble.

Governor Tang turned away from the telescope to face his friends. "It worked," he reported in a daze of relief.

"*Half*-worked," reminded Lucky. "The rescue-rocket never saw us—and we have no way left to signal them or let anyone know we're down here."

"We didn't save ourselves," said Xing-Xing, "but we probably saved everyone else."

Just now the lights snapped off and the cave's electrical system shut down. With the group pulling flashlights from pockets, Mr. Barnett explained:

"I suppose after all these years the batteries couldn't hold a charge."

Lucky pointed his flashlight up under his chin so his companions could see him shaking his head in disgust. "So we're alone," he said, "in the dark, in a cave, on the Moon. Lovely."

They all stood still, not knowing what to do next, a very different scene from the one taking place a hundred feet over their heads, on the surface. Here Byron was doing jumping jacks, which almost always helped him problem-solve. The low lunar gravity was slowing him down to some extent, and the oversized spacesuit was making his jacks fairly floppy, but it was still the best way he knew to make room in his mind for a really good idea to whiz in.

"*Moon to Byron!*" said José Ignacio. "*Come in, Byron!*"

Byron continued his jacks.

"*Hey!*" the robot persisted. "*Sporty von Lunatic! Stop it!*"

This time Byron stopped jumping, but despite his efforts to clear his mind for inspiration, inspiration hadn't come. "*The rescue-rocket'll circle back any minute,*" he said, "*and for all we know, this'll be its last pass! But I still don't know what went wrong with the test fireworks! And if I don't know, I can't fix it! And if I can't fix it, I can't signal the rescue-rocket!"* Optimistically he added: *"Maybe the tester was just a dud and the rest'll work!"*

"Or maybe these fireworks are so old," José Ignacio said, *"that their solid-fuel tubes are decomposing and they need some kind of ballast to make them fly straight."*

Byron knew right away that José Ignacio's idea made sense, that it was his robot who'd had a burst of inspiration. But the implications were troubling.

"Tie the fuses together and hand them to me," José Ignacio said, pointing to the bundle of skyrockets.

"What're you gonna do with them?" Byron did not at all like what he was guessing José Ignacio had in mind.

"My weight will stabilize them. I'LL be the ballast. And if that doesn't work, I can try to keep them on course with bursts from my jets."

This was what Byron had suspected. *"But you'll be too far up to get back!"* he said. *"Inertia won't let you slow down!"*

"That's right. So I'll have to keep going."

"Keep GO-ing?"

"I've been thinking about this for a while now. I don't want to ruffle your feathers, but I believe it's time I went my own way. This is an opportunity for me. I realize you won't like hearing it, but I'm ready to start exploring on my own. Our two-year lease is up next month anyway. I'd only be leaving a little early."

Byron was horror-struck. Not since his very first viewing of *My Teacher Was A Creature* had he felt such a jolt to his vital organs, up to and including his gall bladder. He hadn't mentioned it to José Ignacio yet, but he had every intention of renewing the lease on their human-automaton alliance for another two years. He certainly wasn't ready to cut the contract *short*. But before he could even open his mouth to express himself on the matter, the rescue-rocket appeared in the wild black yonder. This, Byron knew, might well be its very last pass looking for survivors.

"*Hand me the fireworks!*" said José Ignacio.

"No!"

José Ignacio leapt at Byron, to take the fireworks by force. But empowered by the low gravity, Byron knocked the robot back. They fell into battle on the regolith: swinging, punching, pinning, kicking …

"*I can't let you do it!*" hollered Byron.

José Ignacio eventually got the better of his opponent, sitting on him to hold him still. But Byron stretched his hand back over his head, keeping the fireworks just out of reach of José Ignacio's claw. "*I'm not letting you go!*"

"*The thing is,*" said José Ignacio, "*it's not just that I'm ready to start exploring without YOU, but I'm fairly sure you're ready to start exploring without ME.*"

Byron considered it for a second.

"*Let's compromise!*" said José Ignacio. "*Take out my memory bulb!*"

"*But then you won't remember any of this afterwards!*"

"*But YOU will!*"

Byron reflected on this—if too slowly.

"*Hurry!!*" urged José Ignacio. He bent forward so Byron could reach his cranium. Reluctantly, but compelled by the terrible pressure of not losing their last chance to signal the rescue-rocket, Byron unlatched the robot's transparent head, swiveled it open, reached in, and unscrewed José Ignacio's memory bulb, tucking it into a spacesuit pocket for safekeeping.

"*Now hand me those fuses and light 'em up!*" José Ignacio said.

Byron gathered up and handed over the fuses to a dozen individual skyrockets. With swift claw-work, José Ignacio twisted them into a single braid, then held them out for Byron to light. Byron touched the lighter's little flame to the braided fuse and took a step backwards, feeling hopeful and horrible all at once. José Ignacio said:

"*Notwithstanding your egregious personality, your harebrained behavior, and your peculiar ideas concerning which activities make for a pleasant afternoon, I must admit, Byron Barnett, I haven't entirely hated our time together. I have only one thing left to say to you …*"

The lit fuse ignited the fireworks, shooting them into space. José Ignacio took off beneath them using his boot jets, though he was holding tight to the dozen skyrockets by way of their braided fuse—which had conducted the flame into the little skyrockets' fuel tubes without burning up the cord itself. Before he was out of range, José Ignacio transmitted a single word back down to Byron, finishing his parting thought:

"*Zanzibaaaaaaaaaaaaaaar!!!*"

On the regolith below, Byron watched in dismay as the skyrockets started zigzagging wildly—and all twelve in different directions. But José Ignacio compensated by increasing the burn out of his jets, flying up *above* the fireworks, and dragging them back in the right direction: in other words high over the lunar surface.

An unbiased observer, of course, would have seen something different than what Byron had seen: not a seven-foot mechanical man shooting jets out of his boots, but a twelve-inch toy robot attached by cord to the bundled fireworks, its toy-weight providing just enough ballast to stabilize the little skyrockets in flight …

Byron was still gazing into the starry expanse with a sad smile on his face: though he'd no longer be in a position to enjoy his robot's annoying company, he knew for sure now that he'd done the right thing letting José Ignacio go.

Back in Moonbeard Marc's cave, the rest of the group also knew they'd done the right thing by giving something up: in their case giving up the chance to save themselves. They'd used the space-coffin not to signal the rescue-rocket, but to blast the white worm into a state of harmless diamondiferousness and save the Earth instead. Even Lucky von Stroganoff, a selfish so-and-so if ever there was one, had come around to the idea that saving the human race had been a fairly good plan. He was feeling quite calm about it by this time. Standing in the darkened observatory-chamber with the rest of his accidental companions, he slapped his thighs and said:

"Well, I suppose if we're doomed to stay here waiting for the sands of time to run out on the rest of our lives, we may as well see if there's anything in the way of a snack."

He went off to look for the kitchen, using his flashlight to make his way. He wasn't expecting to find anything on the order of a pantry full of Space Gazelle Savories, but it seemed unlikely that Moonbeard Marc had polished off *all* his treats before climbing into that capsule. There had to be *something* lying around that was still edible: some corn chips maybe or a bag of cinnamon thins.

Meanwhile, in the dark of the room behind him, something caught Taji's eye: a tiny burst of color flaring in his peripheral vision, a flicker in the telescope's eyepiece. He leaned in to have a look.

"Something's going on out there."

Xing-Xing came over and leaned into the eyepiece. "I don't believe it!" she said.

"What do you see?" asked her father.

"Fireworks! Going off over the Moon!"

"*Fireworks?* Coming from *where?*"

"I don't know how it's possible, but it looks like they're coming from *us!*"

Mr. Barnett and Mrs. Barnett swung around, aiming their flashlights at the niche of the chamber where Byron was sitting—and saw he was gone. Neither of them knew how he'd done it, but both were sure he'd done *something*. They took turns looking through the telescope's eyepiece, to get a view of the fireworks that were just peaking: big bursts of mint green, neon blueberry, and sizzling pink going off high above the regolith and underneath the icy streak of Comet Khayyam, sending showers of sparks floating back down like so much astral glitter onto the silvery surface of the Moon. The sight of it was practically miraculous, and no less so to Admiral Haddad and Deputy Olaffson in the rescue-rocket, who had the extra if more confusing view of a fireworks-scorched toy robot, twelve inches tall, floating right past the viewport of their ship.

In any case, it was simple enough for these experienced officers of the Astral Corps to zero in on the skyrockets' fire-trails and follow them down to their point of origin. Six minutes later, the Astral Corps' flagship touched down fifty yards from the entrance to Moonbeard Marc's cave. Byron stood there making his presence known, the floppy gloves of his oversized spacesuit especially good for waving a rescue-rocket down to a perfect landing.

CHAPTER: 13

BYRON GUIDED DEPUTY OLAFSSON down to Moonbeard Marc's cave, through the auto-sealant, around the waterfall, past the launch chamber, and into the flashlight-lit lounge where the Tangs, Mrs. and Mr. Barnett, and Lucky were seated in a circle, passing around and slowly snacking on a tin of onion rings that Lucky had found in a vacuum-sealed storage bin. The rings were still acceptably oniony—quite nice for nibbles that were thirty years old.

"Save *me* some!" Byron protested—and to be fair, his stomach *had* been growling for the past half hour while he'd been up on the surface saving everybody by signaling the rescue-rocket.

A scene of some merriment followed. Deputy Olafsson had brought with him a box of spare oxygen-cartridges, the distribution of which now allowed these last refugees from the ravaged city of Cosmopolis to suit up and ascend to the rescue-rocket.

An hour later they were safely ensconced in the main cabin of the Astral Corps' flagship, some of them watching the Earth grow larger out one porthole, some watching the Moon shrink to the size and pale green tint of a honeydew out the other.

Governor Tang, seated with Deputy Olafsson, was sketching on a notepad his ideas for the construction of a new-and-improved Cosmopolis; while Lucky, back in his seat after a long trip to the lavatory, was writing in a notepad of his own. He was composing a letter to his father, including a detailed promise as to how he'd behave more responsibly

now that he was a more mature individual for having survived a slew of lunar traumas and torments. In return, he
hoped that his dear Papa would begin to treat him with a
modicum of respect. Lucky was, let it not be forgotten, his
father's only child—and heir to the von Stroganoff diamond
business to boot. And he was carrying in his pockets the last
lunar diamonds that would make their way down to Earth
for a generation. Diamonds from the cave of Moonbeard
Marc, no less. Stones that would add to the luster of the von
Stroganoff name the way a flashbulb adds to a snapshot.

Just now Taji stepped back into the cabin from the ship's
galley carrying two glasses of fizzy water, one for Xing-Xing,
one for himself. Passing his brother and parents, who were
gazing together out the Moon-side porthole, he paused long
enough to say:

"That's four for four on the saves, Boon. You're a disaster-
magnet on Earth, but on the Moon you're a disaster-*master!*"

Leaving Byron beaming, Taji carried on and took his seat
beside Xing-Xing. As they sipped their fizzy waters, Taji said:

"I'm sorry about Cosmopolis being annihilated and
everything. But don't forget to look on the bright side."

Xing-Xing dropped her jaw and widened her eyes, but
three seconds later she had to smile, despite herself. Taji's
optimism was unbelievable. Who else could even *think* of a
bright side to the obliteration of a lunar colony that had cost
a quadrillion credits and taken twenty years to build?

"Tell me, Taji Lindmark Mwangi Barnett: exactly what
bright side are you referring to?"

"Well, Xing-Xing Francesca Tang, I'm glad you asked. The
bright side I'm referring to is, now that you've been forced to
evacuate the Moon, you'll have me to show you around *my*
home world. It'll be the best date on Earth you've ever had."

"It'll be the *only* date on Earth I've ever had."

"So you'll be starting at the top!"

They carried on this way, taunting and charming each other for the balance of the two hundred and thirty-nine thousand miles of the trip. Meanwhile, a few seats away, Byron was facing a more serious mood with his parents.

"Taji's right," said Mr. Barnett. "On the Moon you *were* a disaster-master. You rescued us from—well, frankly, from certain death, four different times. On the other hand, Byron, you do understand that if you hadn't left your field trip without permission and gone poking around inside Moonbeard Marc's cave, then we wouldn't have had to stay behind to find you and never would've been in danger in the first place."

"Though it's also true," added Mrs. Barnett, "that if we hadn't stayed behind to find you, we never would've discovered the imminent threat posed by the white worm and wouldn't have been in a unique position to stop it before it destroyed the Moon and wreaked havoc on the Earth."

"So on balance," concluded Mr. Barnett, "what your mother and I are saying to you is: nicely done."

His parents were surprised to see that Byron looked ill at ease with the compliment.

"Byron, what's wrong?" said Mrs. Barnett.

"I'm still a *space*-convict!" Byron whispered. "Do you think Judge Monday will let me back into Arizona? I don't want to get re-arrested!"

"We'll ask Governor Tang to put in a good word for you," assured Mr. Barnett. Mrs. Barnett added, only partly in jest:

"Maybe the governor can convince the judge to commute your sentence to a thousand hours of extra violin lessons, after all."

Byron's face twisted into a picture of pain—but before he could speak, Admiral Haddad stepped into the cabin with an important question:

"Byron, would you care to see the cockpit?"

Pain gave way to elation. Byron turned to his mother for permission.

"As long as you give me your solemn promise not to touch anything," she said.

"I promise!"

"Color me skeptical."

"I swear on José Ignacio's claw! I won't touch anything!"

Lucky had been listening in to all this from his seat nearby. He cleared his throat to get the attention of the admiral.

"You can come too, Mr. von Stroganoff."

The boys sprang out of their seats and skedaddled up the aisle and into the cockpit, where Deputy Olafsson was running things from the co-pilot's chair. By the time Admiral Haddad followed a few seconds later, Byron was already hypnotized by the sea of stars out the cockpit's forward window. Then his gaze dropped down to the equally impressive array of dials, levers, lights, and toggles on the cockpit's control-board. He was just about to ask if he could test his grip on the big yellow joystick when an explosion shook the ship, setting off an alarm like a laughing hyena.

Deputy Olafsson consulted his rear-view radar screen. "We've been hit between the fins," he said. "Looks like a debris field from Cosmopolis."

The door to the cockpit flew open, revealing a distraught junior officer. "The rear cabin's on fire!" he reported.

Admiral Haddad reached for the control-board and flipped the switch to the autopilot.

"*Autopilot engaged,*" intoned the ship's computer.

Yanking fire extinguishers off the wall, Admiral Haddad and Deputy Olafsson dashed out the door, though not before the admiral ordered Byron and Lucky:

"You two stay put!"

Left on their own, Lucky plunked himself down in the vacated co-pilot's seat, while Byron took the pilot's seat for himself. They sat in silence for several seconds, until Lucky turned to Byron, who was staring through the window at something out in space. Lucky tried following Byron's gaze. He squinted, but couldn't make it out. "What *is* that?" he asked.

The answer quickly became clearer (and larger) even to Lucky: chunks of blown-up buildings, shattered fragments of domes, tangled masses of wiring and equipment, even a sofa from the lunar living quarters.

"More junk from Cosmopolis," Byron said.

"But why are we heading straight *for* it?!"

"Because we're on autopilot. Destination: Earth, dead ahead."

A new alarm started squealing at them from the control-board, the ship's computer seconding the opinion:

"*Attention! Collision risk! Attention! Collision risk!*"

"We have to *do* something!" said Lucky. "*You* have to do something!

"Me?! I *can't*! I promised mom I wouldn't touch anything!"

"If ever there were a time to break your word, this is it!"

Byron turned to look out the window at the fast approaching debris, then glanced back at the door to the main cabin, then back at the incoming danger out in space. "Give me your hands!" he ordered Lucky.

"My *hands*?! Why?! What are you going to do with them?!"

"I need your hands! Or at least your fingers!"

"My fingers are my fortune! I'm a diamond cutter! I can't live without my digits!"

"And your digits can't live without your body, which is about to be mashed into space-paste! Give me your hands!"

"Tell me why!!"

"I swore I wouldn't touch anything, but I never said *you* wouldn't!"

Lucky thrust out his hands for Byron to do with them what he needed—and Byron swiftly used a borrowed, bony index finger to switch off the autopilot.

"*Autopilot disengaged,*" confirmed the computer.

The ship lurched, sliding the boys off their seats and onto the floor. Byron jumped up first—and saw how close they now were to the debris field. This time he grabbed one of Lucky's hands without asking for it and slapped it down onto the yellow joystick that was now controlling the ship. The blood drained from Lucky's face as his hand was used by Byron to push the joystick down, up, left, down, right, left, up, over ... causing them to zigzag around enormous hunks of space-junk.

Meanwhile, in the rear cabin, Admiral Haddad and her crew were beating back the flames with their fire extinguishers, trying hard to keep their balance despite the ship's spasms ...

Back in the cockpit, Byron jerked the rocket left then right then left one last time to avoid colliding with the final piece of junk in their path: a Space Gazelle vending machine loaded with treats: Cheezy Tidbits, Falafel Nosh, and Pizza Balls, both original and chocolate-dipped. "What a waste," Byron said, shaking his head. The loss of such sublime snacks to the dark void of space was nothing he could pretend indifference to.

After a moment, he released Lucky's hand from the joystick—but had to snatch it back a split-second later to switch the autopilot on again, which he'd almost forgotten.

"*Autopilot engaged,*" the computer intoned.

Byron and Lucky eyed each other. Then Lucky broke out in a big grin. "I didn't vomit," he said.

The door to the main cabin swung open: in came Admiral Haddad and Deputy Olafsson.

"Not to worry, boys," said the admiral. "The fire's out, everything's under control. Though I don't know what all that zigzaggery was about. The autopilot must've been drunk with power."

Byron and Lucky self-ejected from their chairs.

"Thanks for letting us sit up here!" shouted Byron on his way out the door.

"Jolly thoughtful of you, admiral!" added Lucky.

They darted into the main cabin and buckled themselves into their seats without even stopping in the galley to raid the mint bowl.

After surviving the wrath of the white worm and its ramifications, you might think that the four members of the Barnett family would've liked nothing more than to take a catnap for the rest of the ride down to Earth. But that's not the Barnetts. True, Byron himself did doze off for a minute, though even in his sleep he had a lot going on, since he tended to pack a good deal of activity into his dreams.

He'd slipped into the dream that he was dreaming right now while gazing out his window at the Moon dwindling to the size of a marshmallow—and suddenly found himself no longer in the Booniverse at all, but believe it or don't in the José-Ignacioverse! He was on a planet with three moons in a sky as red as a chili pepper, walking through a clifftop park that looked down over a frozen ocean. And he was walking next to José Ignacio, who was only a little over four feet tall, while he, Byron, was seven feet and several centimeters!

All manner of other robots were strolling the park too, many with mechanical pandas on leashes, one with a cybernetic toucan perched on his shoulder. But none of this was the *really* odd part. The *really* odd part, the part that made Byron all of a sudden see things from a whole new point of view, was when José Ignacio's parents met them at the park's snack bar—which instead of selling your typical eatables, your coconut gelato and your fried banana chips, offered treats of a more electronic variety: junction transistors and photovoltaic cells and memory bulbs and whatnot.

José Ignacio's parents were a platinum-plated robotic lady and gentleman. The moment they showed up, they looked *down* at Byron, who in the blink of a kilobyte had shrunk from seven feet and several centimeters to the size of an action figure, which José Ignacio was holding in his claw. What was happening here?!?! Byron was dangling upside-down like somebody's toy, like *José Ignacio's* toy to be perfectly clear about it—and his arms and legs felt like they were made of bendable rubber! Then José Ignacio's parents left to take a stroll to the scenic overlook for a view of the frozen ocean—and Byron was instantly seven feet and several centimeters tall and made of flesh and blood again.

"José Ignacio, what in the name of the eleven deadly realms is going *on*?!"

"What's bothering you now, you preposterous hominid," José Ignacio grumbled.

Byron was truly, practically medically, in shock. He couldn't help wondering if *this*, the José-Ignacioverse, was the reality, and his whole previous life in the Booniverse had been the dream …

—But just now the rescue-rocket hit the Earth's exosphere and Byron popped out of his catnap like a cork out of a champagne bottle. He wasn't ruffled the way you are after waking up from a nightmare, he was stimulated, the way you are when you discover the portal to another dimension behind the khakis hanging in your closet. Gosh, the mind was a complicated body part!

Even more importantly, Byron now realized that he wasn't just a discoverer anymore, he was a philosopher! This opened up a veritable treasure trove of new possibilities: Byron's days as a lunar adventurer might've been over, he admitted to himself, but his years as a mental daredevil were just beginning.

Three seats ahead, Byron's parents were having a little philosophy session of their own.

"Mr. Barnett," said Mrs. Barnett, "I have a proposal for you."

"I accept," said Mr. Barnett.

"Without even hearing it? You really *are* my favorite husband."

"And you're my favorite wife. Now what did I just agree to?"

"Well, I've been thinking: for the past year we've been asking Byron to reflect on his actions and change his ways. But what if we've gotten it backwards? What if we need to reflect on *our* actions and change *our* ways."

"Hmm. Not sure I'm following. Would you be kind and elaborate?"

"Certainly. We've been telling Byron to stop using his imagination as an excuse for bad behavior, but maybe the message should've been to start using his imagination as a launching pad for *good* behavior."

"I like what I'm hearing. Go on."

"Let's tell the truth: our son has a very strange brain, the source of his many odd ideas and any number of unusual perspectives. Which is either a sign of future glory or a recipe for lifelong disaster."

"Agreed. So what do you have in mind?"

"We need to help him apply his imagination toward less fictitious and more factual ends."

"I concur."

"But my feeling is, we can only manage that if we spend more time with him, and we can only spend more time with him ..."

Mrs. Barnett paused. Mr. Barnett had to ask:

"Yes?"

" ... if you quit your job and I quit mine."

"*What*?!"

"We need to quit our jobs—and go into business together."

"I can hardly believe what I'm hearing! You want me to leave Amalgamated MegaPhysics?"

"Why not? We could start a company of our own."

"An engineering company, you mean?"

"A *family* engineering company."

"Wait! I already have a name for it! 'Barnetts Build It Better Incorporated.' 'BBIB' for short."

"Wallace, that's *perfect*."

"But are you sure you're ready to dive back into the engineering biz full-time?"

"I really am. Reconfiguring that space-coffin made me realize how much I miss it."

"Well, I don't deny that before the boys came along, my favorite part of going to AmPhys every day was seeing *you* there. It's never been the same since you left."

"So quit."

"But if you quit your job too …" Mr. Barnett mused.

"… we'll have to hire a housekeeper, a cook, an accountant, and a personal assistant," Mrs. Barnett said, finishing her husband's sentence. "Plus we'll need a plumber, an electrician, and a glazier on call."

"I've never known how you did all those things anyway," Mr. Barnett confessed.

"Also a kitchen technician for when the scanning electron oven goes on the blink, a nurse on call, and a gardener and undergardener to keep my backyard from falling into ruin."

"Golly. Can we afford all that?"

"If we make the new company a success we can."

Mr. Barnett liked this: it was just the kind of challenge he'd secretly been dreaming of for more than a little while now.

"So we'll quit our jobs," Mrs. Barnett recapped, "then we'll officially start up BBIB. We'll build an addition to the house for office and studio space, we'll work from home, and every day after school Byron can work *with* us for an hour or two. He's about to be ten years old: now is our moment to help him focus his energies and find his way forward. If he wants to build a robot, we'll teach him how to build a *real* robot. If he wants to build a particle accelerator, we'll teach him how to build a *real* particle accelerator. If he wants to build a spacetime disruptor, we'll teach him how to build another robot."

"Love it," Mr. Barnett said. "Love, love, love, love, love."

Not many parents would change for their children instead of making their children change for *them*, but the Barnetts were not like most people. They were, however, exactly like themselves. It was about to give Byron the leg up in life that he didn't even realize he needed.

CHAPTER: 14

SOME STORIES END UP right where you think they will. Others swerve at the last minute to someplace you'd never have guessed. To get to where *this* story ends, we'll have to weave our way through certain events happening thirty whole years *after* Admiral Haddad's rescue-rocket delivered Byron safely back to Earth. Thirty years, four months, five days, and a couple of nanoseconds, to be exact.

But let's not get stuck on the numbers. Because this is the moment to rev yourself up for a change of perspective, make sure your shoes are tied, look spacetime straight in the eye, and take a giant leap into the future.

Like so:

"—and we have liftoff!!!!!!!!!!!!!!"

The voice of Archer Overly, Science Correspondent for the Lunar News Service, boomed through every speaker across the shining city of New Cosmopolis, or "New Coz" to say it the way Lunarites and Lunarians referred to their off-Earth home.

This was no ordinary liftoff. All eyes across the city were fixed through windows and scopes on a golden space-craft now leaving the North Landing Zone: a circular, ultramodern vessel that wasn't blasting into space with the flame, smoke, and roar of an old-fashioned atomic rocket, but rising effortlessly into the black velvet of the cosmos on the power of original thinking. In seconds it was high over this rebuilt Cosmopolis, a city five times larger than the old Cosmopolis destroyed in the legendary White Worm Calamity three decades earlier.

Inside the Command Tower, Archer Overly stood speaking before a broadcast camera, his report beaming not only to every screen in the city but to several billion screens back on Earth:

"And *The Zanzibar* is up and away. So begins the maiden voyage of this first of the new class of galactic-caliber spacecraft, bearing inside it another first: the first family of explorers to venture beyond our solar system."

Telescreens were intercutting between three shots: the golden-hulled *Zanzibar* picking up speed as it moved away from the Moon; Archer Overly continuing his report from the control room atop the municipal tower; and a live view of the interior of *The Zanzibar*, transmitted back via on-board cameras. The ship's complement numbered four persons, all strapped into seats in the bridge of their roomy spaceship.

Archer Overly continued:

"Led by Captain Boon Barnett, architect of the Astral Corps' long-range exploration program, *The Zanzibar*'s very special crew is filled out by Dr. Honeybun Bajpai, ship's physician and not-so-coincidentally married to Captain Barnett, along with their ten-year-old boys: Vishram and Virgilio, the Bajpai-Barnett twins. Also on board is an extraordinary invention of Captain Barnett's, the fruit of a decade's labor: his mechanical assistant and *The Zanzibar*'s all-around handyman, the so-called 'robotic prodigy' of the Astral Corps: 'Igna.' But it's *The Zanzibar* itself, or more precisely *The Zanzibar*'s revolutionary, lepton-powered engine, that represents Captain Barnett's greatest achievement and indeed is the breakthrough that with this liftoff will forever change the nature of space travel by immeasurably lengthening humankind's reach into the cosmic deep."

Since Archer Overly's job was not only to narrate the liftoff for his viewing audience but more generally to fill up airtime for this live news broadcast, he now spent several minutes describing how Captain Barnett had thought up the lepton engine as a mere boy and developed the concept alongside his parents at their family engineering company, Barnetts Build It Better Incorporated.

Though well-informed, Mr. Overly did not possess *all* the facts of the matter. For instance: he was unaware that it was on the very night they returned to Arizona after their disastrous day on the Moon that Mr. and Mrs. Barnett told the boys they planned to quit their jobs and start working from home. Nor did Mr. Overly know that Byron then immediately announced that what he wished to work on alongside his parents at home was a spaceship. And not just any old spaceship, but a spaceship that could travel if possible interdimensionally, though at the very least intergalactically. He'd already jotted down a variety of ideas for just such a vehicle, many of which his parents could tell on quick inspection were quite kooky and unlikely to pan out, but one of which, once his parents helped him harness the power of his own deep kook, proved promising.

Add to this thirty years and fifty-thousand-odd hours of trial and error in the BBIB labs, plus the insights gleaned from Byron's eventual education at the Arizona Institute of Technology, and his lepton-engine actually, amazingly, world-changingly, worked.

Here Mr. Overly smiled into the lens of the camera. "I have a surprise now not only for our viewing audience, but for Captain Barnett himself. I believe the Command Tower has patched me through. Captain Barnett? Do you read me?"

From loudspeakers on the Moon and on screens across every continent on Earth came Byron's voice, the voice not of a boy as we first knew him, but a man who, if all went according to plan, would be celebrating his forty-first, forty-second, and forty-third birthdays while zipping through intergalactic space.

"*Reading you loud and clear, Mr. Overly. How's the view of 'The Zanzibar' from down there?*"

"That is one magnificent-looking spaceship you've built, Captain Barnett."

"*Ah, well, our team leader on this ship's design was actually my magnificent mother. So ... nice job, mom!*"

Mrs. Barnett was at this very moment seated across the breakfast table from Mr. Barnett, at their same house of stacked glass polygons in Arizona. Mr. Barnett was breakfasting on blueberry pancakes, Mrs. Barnett on cottage cheese and ripe cherries. They smiled at each other hearing Byron's voice transmitted all the way down to them from outer space and through their telescreen. When Byron paid his mother that well-deserved compliment about *The Zanzibar*'s design, Mr. Barnett reached over the salt and pepper shakers, took his wife's hand, and kissed it.

"Mr. Barnett," scolded Mrs. Barnett, "there's no need to get frisky before nine a.m."

Mr. Barnett stood up from his seat, pulled Mrs. Barnett up out of hers, and started kissing her cheeks and her forehead and her nose and then her elbows over and over and over, so many times that Mrs. Barnett broke out laughing. It was a very memorable breakfast.

Back on the Moon, Archer Overly said to Byron by radio transmission: "Well, I'm glad you brought up the subject of your talented family, Captain Barnett, because that leads me to a surprise that's been months in the making. The Lunar League has commissioned a special sendoff for you and your mission from the space-artist known as 'Mwangi.' And what our viewing and listening audience may not know is that Mwangi is in fact Taji Lindmark Mwangi Barnett, your own brother."

Indeed, in the three decades since his day on the Moon, Taji had gone on to become one of the most famous space-artists in the world. From teenage photographer's assistant to art school student to portrait artist to *space* portrait artist: this was the path he'd taken. With his parents' help he'd invented a kind of super-charged laser that allowed him to temporarily project a person's picture out into space and onto celestial objects such as asteroids or meteoroids or in some cases icy comets.

For one very expensive commission, he'd even lasered a whole family's faces onto the moons of Jupiter. People loved these so-called "ephemeral projections"—they only lasted a week, but it was super-fun to look through a telescope during those seven days and see your face or your sweetie's on a rock flying through the solar system or to surprise your girlfriend with her visage on a comet and sometimes even to use it as a way to propose marriage to her (or her to him) or to buy your mom and dad a space portrait for their twenty-fifth wedding anniversary so they and all their friends could step outside after cutting the cake at the party and admire themselves in the night sky. Nobody, it turns out, doesn't like to see their face in space.

Evolving as an artist, Mwangi had eventually given up using people as the subject of his artwork and moved into environmental space-art. His most famous works were: *Lunar Ladders*, a series of giant pink ladders planted upright in long rows at the bottom of Crater Copernicus ... and *Moon Wrap*, where he wrapped the rubble of the original Cosmopolis in a bright purple plastic sheet a mile wide. And though he'd made his fortune on the space portraits, he now made his reputation with these installations. The art critics went wild over them. *The Lunar Times* wrote:

> With *Moon Wrap* Mwangi has given us a way to look at our past and our future at the same time: a thrilling reinterpretation of physical destruction as a tableau not only of hope, but beauty. Mwangi is, in the final analysis, a visionary teaching us to see the familiar in gorgeously unfamiliar ways.

Pre-arranged by the Lunar News Service, Taji, speaking into a microphone and transmitter relay set up in his studio in New Cosmopolis, now communicated directly with his brother on *The Zanzibar*:

"Boon, this is Taji. How's it going up there?"

"Hey, T-Bar, nice to hear from you. What's it been, three hours since I saw you at the waffle station? Missing me already?"

Here Archer Overly interjected:

"Just remember, gentlemen, we have three billion people listening in. So nothing *too* personal."

Taji said to his brother:

"Boon, you remember that ZipperCon I took you to a few months before you turned ten? Where I bought you that false-color poster of the Moon that you wanted? The one where the Moon wasn't gray and white but all kinds of colors to help the eye make out the topography?"

"Sure."

"And you were possibly going to pay me back out of your allowance because I was saving up for a hoverpod? But a year later you renegotiated and gave me the poster instead?"

"That sounds like me."

"Well, I took that poster with me to art school and hung it over my bed, then I hung it on the wall in my first studio, then my second, and finally next to the picture window in my studio here on the Moon. And eventually I started to see what you saw in it: a different way of looking at things."

"Nice!"

"So with that in mind, I have a surprise for you. I've been working with the Lunar League over the past few months to send up a series of very special, laser-projecting satellites that we've now got circling the Moon. Look out your aft viewport."

Aboard *The Zanzibar* Boon did as his brother asked: he swiveled to look out the aft viewport, meaning the window that offered a view of the Moon that was growing smaller with every passing moment but was still big enough to see Cosmopolis itself and all the major craters. Just now Taji flipped a switch in his studio connected by microwave to the series of laser-projecting satellites that he'd mentioned, triggering their beams ...

... and:

"Rabiznaz!" Boon blurted as the Moon's silvery normalness switched to a jelly-bean-jar medley of fluorescent strawberry, unusually bold purple, shiny turquoise, the brightest of lemon yellows, pale pistachio green, vivid tangerine, and popsicle blue.

"Taji! ... I can't believe it! It's ... it's an absolute MASTERpiece!"

Boon was right. Taji's *Moon Wrap* and *Lunar Ladders* notwithstanding, this was his greatest work of art yet. Quite possibly the greatest work of art of all time. Certainly the best sendoff that any artist could ever give to his intergalactically traveling brother.

But it almost hadn't happened. Two weeks earlier, a Lunar League councilmember had complained that sending up special satellites so that Mwangi could laser the Moon in crazy colors as a going-away present for his own brother was an inappropriate use of public funds. It was a private present, he said; it should be paid for privately. Using private satellites. So the whole thing was vetoed and called off.

Fortunately the Governor of the Moon had different thoughts on the matter. She issued an executive order vetoing the veto. Mwangi's *Lunar Super Color Booster* was back on. In a written statement, the governor explained that temporarily turning the Moon into a work of art for *The Zanzibar's* sendoff would be a gift not only to Captain Barnett, but to all humanity.

Indeed, right now and all week long, for everybody on Earth looking up at the night sky and seeing a moon not like the Moon they knew from real life but like a moon out of their wildest dreams, it was nothing less than a gift par excellence. It made billions of people happy seeing that jelly-beaned orb in the heavens for the next seven days. Every human on every continent had a different view of the night sky for a while, a new view, a *joyful* view—and therefore a new view of life. What better gift is there than that?

The Governor of the Moon had been exactly right. Wow, she was smart! The Lunarians and Lunarites who'd voted her into office, making her their very first governor whose own father had been governor too, really knew what they were doing. Xing-Xing Tang was already one of the best governors they'd ever had—and she was only getting started. From her office atop the command center in New Cosmopolis, she was high enough to look down and see with her own eyes various sections of the regolith lasered fluorescent strawberry and unusually bold purple, even without glancing at her tele-screen that was now broadcasting a live shot of the Moon as seen through the big telescope at Hawaii's Kumaka-poipoi Observatory.

Captain Barnett, looking out the aft viewport of *The Zanzibar*, was still enjoying Taji's *Lunar Super Color Booster* too. The false-color view of the Moon that Byron had bought at ZipperCon as a boy had become the *real*-color view of the Moon—at least for a while. It was a beautiful way to exit the solar system.

Soon *The Zanzibar* went whizzing past Mars ... and the Moon slipped behind the Earth through the viewport; so Boon swiveled forward again and smiled at his wife, who gave him a wink of approval. Boon turned to Vishram and Virgilio to pass the wink along to them, but they were busy telling each other knock-knock jokes, so Boon decided not to interrupt. All the lights on his instrument panel were green, his family was happy, and he was on his way to explore a new galaxy. He was, as he liked to call himself when things were going well, a content Barnett.

Twenty-two minutes later, the ship reached cruising velocity. While zipping around the rings of Saturn, the crew unstrapped themselves from their seats, moved across to the roomy lounge, settled onto upholstered green-leather benches, and—and this may surprise some people to hear—started playing Tchaikovsky. The Barnett Family was also a string quartet! Captain Barnett, as was well known through-out the Astral Corps, was nearly as brilliant a violinist as he was a pilot and engineer; Dr. Bajpai was likewise an accomplished violinist and could also hold her own on the flute; Vishram was the family cellist; and Virgilio played the viola—though he was just as good on clarinet.

With Igna on the bridge keeping watch—this was one of the robot's primary functions: autopilot oversight and backup navigation system—the Barnetts were free to play their music, launching into Tchaikovsky's string quartet No. 1 in D Major: the perfect soundtrack for galactic travel in Captain Barnett's opinion. Back on Earth and the Moon, eyes were still glued to telescreens, with billions of people watching and now listening to these astronaut-musicians carry some of the finest melodies ever written into the cosmic deep. Then the transmission switched back to the Command Tower at New Cosmopolis, where Archer Overly told his audience:

"More on the flight of *The Zanzibar* in just a moment, but first a brief word from our sponsor."

Lucky von Stroganoff popped up on everybody's telescreens: older than when we last saw him, but looking, sounding, and acting even more Stroganoffian than before. (Or is that more Stroganoffesque?) He wore a French musketeer's feathered hat and a purple velvet outfit studded with diamonds in place of buttons. He looked directly at the camera with a mysterious smile while a narrator said in an accent that no one listening could quite place:

"Whether in London, Beijing, Miami or Mumbai, those in the know go to Lucky von Stroganoff for the gemstones they need to make life sparkle."

Lucky extended his purple-gloved hand, revealing in his palm a big, gleaming diamond ring. "When you're ready for the best," he said, "you're ready for a Stroganoff."

He wasn't exaggerating. Stroganoff diamonds were the most unique gemstones not only on Earth, but in the entire universe. Now you might be thinking: "Isn't every diamond the same on the inside as every other diamond?" The answer is: "Not if it's a diamond chipped off a frozen white worm, it's not."

Here's how it happened:

Six years after the calamity on the Moon, Lucky's father, Julius von Stroganoff, retired—and Lucky took over the family business. And for six years after that, Lucky had one thing in mind: get back to that worm!

Of course it was a fantastically expensive proposition, and no bank would lend him the money to try. So he took a risk. He brought in a business partner, one Rufus van der Burger, a space-entrepreneur with the cash that Lucky needed. Rufus spent a hundred million credits on the plan, which is a real gob of cash, no matter how much you have in your account. In return, Lucky put up the deed to his own house in London, plus his Pablo Picasso painting, *Lady With An Emerald Necklace*, plus a controlling stake in the Stroganoff company itself.

If the plan failed, he'd lose nearly everything. But he couldn't think about that for now; he could only think about how to get the job done. So with Rufus's money, he hired Barnetts Build It Better to construct a very special space probe, which they did for him in eighteen months, in record time. Then he bought a used rocket-ship from the Astral Corps (which ate up a quite a chunk of Rufus's hundred million) and sent the rocket out to where the white worm was drifting, just this side of the icy objects of the Kuiper belt, right past Neptune. At first he'd tried to be economical about it and *rent* a rocket from the Astral Corps, but they pointed out that the rocket wouldn't have enough fuel to fly home from the mining mission Lucky was contemplating. So it was going to have to be a purchase situation.

No one predicted that Lucky's rocket would make it all the way out to the frozen white worm, aka the "Diamond Worm" as it's known today in all the space literature. No one believed that BBIB's probe would detach from the rocket as scheduled, much less land on the Diamond Worm successfully. No one imagined that this intricate and untested equipment would perform its robotic mining operation flawlessly, collect a hundred pounds of stones, take off again using its own return-thrusters, fly through the solar system back to Earth, and parachute into the Indian Ocean all in one piece.

But it turns out that Lucky *was* lucky, after all. On top of which, he had business savvy! His risk had paid off, and he was now the owner of the rarest stones in recorded history, which he turned into some of the most beautifully cut and polished gemstones in recorded history, which made for jewelry that was literally out of this world.

When other space-entrepreneurs teamed up with other jewelers and asked BBIB to build similar probes with similarly special mining technology, Mr. and Mrs. Barnett, out of loyalty to Lucky, always said no. (He'd become something of a third son to them over the years—or at least a favorite nephew.) The Barnetts were asked many times as a matter of fact, but each and every time they declined to build another such device, no matter how many credits they were offered to take the job. So the Diamond Worm, a mass of carbon atoms bonded together in the largest tetrahedral lattice in all creation as far as anybody knows, kept drifting farther out in space and time, un-landed-on and un-mined by any other probe from Earth, ever again.

Meanwhile, Lucky and Rufus became quite the pair. They went on to many successes together, personal and professional. They even founded a mentoring organization in their spare time, called The Club For Kids Who Tend To Vomit In Space, to teach Earth-related leadership skills to boys and girls who weren't super-interested in astronomy, rocket-ships, or black holes. Which is a bit ironic coming from the man for whom outer space had done so much—but that was Lucky.

— "And we're back!" said Archer Overly as the transmission switched from the end of the von Stroganoff commercial to the Command Tower again. Archer knew he was the reporter with the best story of the decade as he told his audience of billions:

"It's been a real treat, hasn't it ladies and gentlemen, watching the launch of the most important space mission in a generation. We who remain behind wish this brave crew of explorers Godspeed as they take the next giant step along the path of human history. To the Family Bajpai-Barnett then, on behalf of the family of women, men, and children of the Earth and Moon, this is Archer Overly for the Lunar News Service, saying: Bon Voyage!"

That night, as telescreens on the Moon and around the Earth were turned off for bedtime, aboard *The Zanzibar* it was also the end of a long day …

Captain Barnett, "Byron" as we knew him way back when but our own "Boon" today, had tucked in the twins; his wife was relaxing in a bubble bath in *The Zanzibar's* luxurious soaking tub, the installation of which had been Honeybun's one condition for agreeing to take her family into intergalactic space; and the robot, Igna, was powering down for his Day One Diagnostic.

Boon had a moment to himself. He might've gazed out one of the ship's many viewports at a starscape that no human eye had beheld before his, but despite his taste for

maximum travel, he'd learned over time that the sights in*side*
oneself were also worth exploring on a regular basis. So he
went into his ready room and picked up a small balsa wood
box that he'd carved when he was about Vishram and Virgilio's
age. Opening it, he ran a finger over:

* ✳ a ticket stub to what was still his all-time favorite
  movie, *My Teacher Was A Creature*;

* ✳ a pair of von Stroganoff diamond cufflinks that
  Lucky had given him on his wedding day;

* ✳ a dried leaf from the sub-lunar palace of
  J. Marcus Mingus;

* ✳ the foil wrapper from a Space Cake:
  Venusian Vanilla;

* ✳ and a tiny light bulb from the cranium of a
  toy robot he once knew.

He held the bulb between thumb and index finger, lifted it
up to examine its burned-out filament, and, letting pictures
brim in his brain of that outstanding day on the Moon all that
time ago, he remembered everything …

                                              …

                        …

                                       …

… which is where Boon's story *might* have finished up. A nice,
ordinary ending for a nice, ordinary evening in outer space.
Except that the ordinary is often an illusion while the hard-
to-believe can be absolute fact. And the absolute fact in this
instance was that, as Boon now levered the seatback of his
reclining chair to a more comfy, half-horizontal position,
he glanced out the room's viewport—and saw something
seriously weird.

He un-reclined, stood up, plucked his hyper-scope off its wall mount, aimed it at the viewport, put his eye to the eye-piece, dialed the magnification to maximum ... and saw his own face in the cosmic deep! Not his current forty-year-old face, but his ten-year-old face from thirty years ago: super-huge on the head of a passing comet! (It looked not unlike one of his brother's space-portraits, those "ephemeral projections" that had made Taji one of the most famous artists on Earth. But Earth was already multiple millions of miles away: way too far for Taji to be the responsible party behind *this* projection.)

Even weirder was that, *in* the projection, Byron wasn't frozen like a snapshot, he was moving like a movie. Adult Boon watched as his ten-year-old self, giant-sized on the head of an interstellar ice ball, raised up a sign made from a square of white poster board.

Scribbled on it in neon green magic marker, in what Boon recognized as his very own handwriting from the elementary school years, were the words:

BYRON TO BOON!
CODE: COCONUT!

Suddenly the projection ceased: ten-year-old Byron was gone, and the comet on which he'd appeared came streaking past *The Zanzibar* like a regular celestial object. Outer space looked outer-spacious again, as per normal.

Adrenaline burst from the relevant glands in Boon's body, rippling up to his scalp and down to his toes. Why, specifically? Because the message on the poster board had come straight out of his top secret code-book from the Nomad in the Ninth Dimension years, ages eight through twelve. "Code: Coconut!" meant "Timeline Disruption!"

This could be bad. Timeline disruptions were wildly dangerous. Whatever was causing this one—a spatial spasm maybe or some kind of galactic glitch—had to be fixed fast or it might just bring existence and/or reality to an end. Still, Boon couldn't help smiling about it just a little. Because if ever somebody was born to take on a repair job of cosmic proportions, it was—if he did say so himself—himself. He'd just need a little more info before getting started.

Dashing out of his ready room, he zipped into the hallway and leapt down the ship's circular staircase, heading for the family quarters to see if the boys were asleep yet and whether Honeybun was still in the tub. A development at the "Code: Coconut" level was not the kind of news you hung on to until morning.

At the same time, thirty years earlier, ten-year-old Byron was now sneaking downstairs when he should've been in bed with lights out. Fully dressed but carrying his sneakers, he tiptoed in socks past the den where his parents and Taji were glued to the telescreen, then he slid like a speed skater down the long hallway to the kitchen.

Here, in the pantry, he quickly filled a knapsack with supplies: a bag of dried pineapple rings, a box of Space Gazelle Cheezy Tidbits, a jar of honey-glazed pecans, a dozen sticks of gum, and a variety pack of Space Cakes for astronomical energy. He also took a bag of chocolate-covered pretzels and a bag of pretzel rods with chocolate filling—because only a fool sets out to fix a glitch in the galaxy without a snack or two.

FOR MORE ON BOON, VISIT:
www.BoonOnTheMoon.space
www.TheBooniverse.space